I0661000

Madison Julius Cawein

Intimations of the Beautiful

Madison Julius Cawein

Intimations of the Beautiful

ISBN/EAN: 9783743311688

Manufactured in Europe, USA, Canada, Australia, Japa

Cover: Foto ©Andreas Hilbeck / pixelio.de

Manufactured and distributed by brebook publishing software
(www.brebook.com)

Madison Julius Cawein

Intimations of the Beautiful

Madison Julius Cawein

Intimations of the Beautiful

BY THE SAME AUTHOR.

DAYS AND DREAMS	$1.25
MOODS AND MEMORIES	2.00
RED LEAVES AND ROSES	1.25
POEMS OF NATURE AND LOVE . . .	1.50
INTIMATIONS OF THE BEAUTIFUL . . .	1.50

G. P. PUTNAM'S SONS

INTIMATIONS OF THE BEAUTIFUL

AND

POEMS

BY

MADISON CAWEIN

G. P. PUTNAM'S SONS

NEW YORK
27 West Twenty-third Street

LONDON
24 Bedford Street, Strand

The Knickerbocker Press

1894

TO

THE AUTHOR OF

"GOD IN HIS WORLD"

WITH

PROFOUND ADMIRATION

They took him into confidence—each oak
  Of the far forest : and all day he sat
  Hearing of Nature from an autocrat,
An oak—so old, Dodona might have spoke
Its infant oracles through it—that, part
  Of the oracular beauty of the gods,
Yet irresponsible, down in its heart
  Still felt the rapture of their periods.

They took him into confidence—the skies :
  And all night long he lay beneath one star,
  Hearing of God . . . One that was chorister
At Earth's first morning ; that beheld fierce eyes
Of rebel angels, and the birth of Hell ;
  Whom God set over Eden and o'er them,
The two, as destiny ; that did foretell
  How Christ lay born at far-off Bethlehem.

CONTENTS.

INTIMATIONS OF THE BEAUTIFUL.

A THOUGHT, to lift me up to those
    Sweet wildflowers of the pensive woods ;
    The lofty, lowly attitudes
Of bluet and of bramble-rose :
    To lift me where the mind may reach
    The lessons that their beauties teach.

A dream, to lead my spirit on
    In sounds of fairy shawms and flutes,
    And all mysterious attributes
Of skies of dusk and skies of dawn :
    To lead me, like the dreamy brooks,
    Past all the knowledge of the books.

A song, to make my heart a guest
    Of happiness whose soul is love ;
    One with the life that knoweth of

But song that turneth toil to rest :
　　To make me cousin to the birds,
　　Whose music needs not wisdom's words.

I.

I feel thee,—as one feels a flower's,
A dead flower's, fragrance in a room,—
A dim, gray grief that haunts the hours
　　　　With sad perfume.

Thou charm'st me,—as a ghostly lily
Might charm a garden's withered place,—
With the pale pathos and the chilly
　　　　Hush of thy face.

I hearken in thy fogs ; I hearken
Ere, like the ghastly ghost of Night,
With immaterial limbs they darken
　　　　The day with white.

With wrecks of rain and mad winds, heaping
Red ruins of riven rose and leaf,

Make glad my heart, O Autumn, sweeping
   The joy with grief.

II.

The gods of Greece are mine once more !
   The old philosophies again !
For I have drunk the hellebore
   Of dreams, and dreams have made me sane—
The wine of dreams ! that doth unfold
   My other self,—'mid shadowy shrines
Of myths which marble held of old,
Part of the Age of Bronze or Gold,—
   That lives a pagan 'mid the pines.

Dead myths, to whom such dreams belong !
   O beautiful philosophies
Of Nature ! crystallized in song
   And marble, peopling lost seas,
Lost forests and the star-lost vast,
   Grant me the childlike faith that clung,—
Through loveliness that could not last,—
To Heaven in the pagan past,
   Calling for God with infant tongue !

III.

Idea, O god of Plato ! one
　With beauty, justice, truth and love :
Who, type by type, the world begun
　From an ideal world above !
Reason, who into Nature wrought
　Your real entities,—which are
　Ideas,—giving to our star
Their beauty through reflected thought ;

The reminiscences, that flame
　Momental through the mind of man,
Of things his memory cannot name
　Lost things his knowledge cannot scan,
Hints of past periods, are not these ?
　His soul hath lived since it had birth
　From God . . . Yea, who shall name the Earth
More ancient than himself who sees ?

IV.

Beside us, and yet far above,
　She leads us to no base renown—
　The Ideal, with her sun-white crown,

And starry raiment of her love :
She leads us by ascending ways
   Of Nature to her purposed ends,
Who in the difficult, dark days
   Of trial with her smile defends.

Beyond the years, that blindly grope,
   To climb with her, from year to year,
   To some exalted atmosphere,
Were more than earthly joy and hope !
Though in that atmosphere we find
   Not her—her influence, pointing to
New elevations of the mind
   By some superior avenue.

v.

The climbing-cricket in the dusk
   Moves wings of moony gossamer ;
   Its vague, vibrating note I hear
Among the boughs of dew and musk,
Whence, rustling with a mellow thud,
   The ripe quince falls. Low, deep and clear,
The west is bound with burning blood.

The slanting bats beneath the moon,—
　　A dark disk edged with glittering white,—
　　Spin loops of intertangled night :
An owl wakes, hooting over soon,
Within the forest far away :
　　And now the heaven fills, light by light,
And all the blood-red west grows gray.

I hear no sound of wind or wave ;
　　No sob or song, except the slow
　　Leaf-cricket's flute-soft tremolo,
Among wet walks grown gray and grave.—
In raiment mists of silver sear,
　　With strange, pale eyes thou comest, O
Thou spirit of the waning year !

VI.

The hills are full of prophecies
　　And ancient voices of the dead ;
Of hidden shapes that no one sees,
Pale, visionary presences,
　　That speak the things no tongue hath said,
　　No mind hath thought, no eye hath read.

The streams are full of oracles,
   And momentary whisperings ;
An immaterial beauty swells
Its breezy silver o'er the shells
   With wordless speech that sings and sings
   The present life of unknown things.

No indeterminable thought is theirs,
   The stars, the sunsets and the flowers ;
Whose inexpressible speech declares
Th' immortal Beautiful, who shares
   This mortal riddle that is ours,
   Beyond the forward flying hours.

VII.

The hornet stings the garnet grape,
   Whose hull splits with the honeyed heat ;—
   Fall hears the long loud locust beat
Its song out, where, a girl-like shape,
   She watches through the wine-press' crust
   Sweet trickle of the purple must.

The bee clings to the scarlet peach,
  That thrusts a dryad's cheek between
  The leaves of golden gray and green ;—
Fall walks where orchard branches reach
  Abundance to her hands, or drop
  Their ripeness down to make her stop.

The bitter-sweet and sassafras
  Hang yellow seeds and crimson-black
  Along the rails, that ramble back
Among the corn where she must pass ;
  Where, on her hair, a golden haze
  Showers the pollen of the maize.

Not till 'mid sad, chill scents all day
  The green leaf-cricket lisps its tune,
  And underneath the hunter's-moon
The oxen plod through clinging clay,
  Or when beyond the dripping pane
  The night sets in with whirling rain :

Not till ripe walnuts spill their spice .
  Of frost-nipped nuts down, and the oak

Pelts with brown acorns, stroke on stroke,
The creek which slides through hints of ice ;
And in the lane the wagon pulls,
Crunching, through thick-strewn hickory hulls :

Not till through frosty fogs, which hold
Wet mornings with their phantom night,
Like torches glimmering through the white,
The woods burn crimson blurs and gold,
And through the mist come muffled sounds
Of hunting-horns and baying hounds :

Shall I on hills, where looming pines
Against vermilion sunsets stand—
Black ruins in a blood-red land—
In wrecks of sumach and wild vines,
Go seek her, where she lies asleep,
Her dark, sad eyes too tired to weep.

VIII.

It holds and beckons in the streams ;
It lures and touches us in all
The flowers of the golden fall—

The mystic essence of our dreams :
A nymph blows bubbling music where
　　Faint water ripples down the rocks ;
　　A faun goes dancing hoiden locks,
And piping some Pandean air,
Through trees the instant wind shakes bare.

Our dreams are never otherwise
　　Than real if they hold us so ;
　　We in some other life shall know
Them parts of it and recognize
Them as ideal substance, whence
　　The actual is—(as flowers and trees,
　　From color sources no one sees,
Draw dyes, the substance of a sense)—
Material with intelligence.

IX.

Once more I watch the hills take fire
　　In dawn ; and shaggy spine by spine,
　　Flush like dark tyrants o'er their wine,
Who grasp the sword and smite the lyre,

And carve the world to their desire ;
  While red as blocks where kingdoms bleed,
  The rocks trail savage vine and weed.

To walls of gold, Enchantment built,
  Again my fancy bids me go—
  Through woods, bewitched with fire, that blow
Wild horns of tournament and tilt—
A fairy prince, whose spear hath spilt
  No blood but in a shadow-world,
  While at the real his gauge was hurled.

What far, æolian echoes lead
  My longing ?—as a voice might wake
  A lost child from deep sleep and take,
With music of a magic reed,
Him home where love shall give him heed :—
  What echoes, blown from lands that lie
  Melodious 'neath no mortal sky ?

X.

The fire, to which the Magi prayed,
  The Aztecs sacrificed and kneeled,

Whose ceremonies now are sealed,
Whose priests are dust, whose people weighed,
Since God permitted such, should man,—
All ignorant of heavenly ends,—
Despise the means, since Earth began,
He works by to perfect His plan,
Which through immediate forms ascends
Of Nature, lifting, race by race,
Man to the beauty of His face ?

Through Nature only we arrive
At God : identical with truth,
By periods of repeated youth,
Through Nature must the Ages strive ;
The Epochs, that must purify
Themselves through her experience,
Her knowledge, which each Age lays by
To clothe it better for the sky
In robes of new intelligence
Befitting life, that upwardly
Approaches ends but God can see.

XI.

Within the life awake behold
　A life asleep　.　.　.　the wildwood shades !
With limbs of glimmering coolness lolled
Along the purple forest glades :—
　Sleep in each unremembering face,
The sea-worn Greeks knew these of old—
　Day's languid lotus-eating race.

Within the mind asleep I mark
　A mind awake ; and see the sense
That stirs the sap beneath the bark
　With tender hints of violence,
　The liquid germs of leaf and bud,
And in the ponderable dark
　Fulfils the offices of blood.

O wiser than Thy works !—behind
　Thy works,—who shall behold Thy place ?
Beyond the suns whose beams burn blind
　Before the glory of Thy face !—

Among the least of these, shall we
Presume to give to Thee, defined,
  A place and personality !

XII.

Across the hills, that roll and rise
Beneath the blue, adoring skies,
  Maturing Beauty by the old,
Fierce forest stands, as might a slave
Before a Sultan sitting grave,
  Grim-gazing from a throne of gold.

Across the hills, that rise and fall,
I gaze with eyes grown spiritual,
  And see the spirit of the dew
From out the morn, that stains the mist
With amber and with amethyst,
  Blown bubble-bright along the blue.

What king such kingly pomp can show
As on the hills the afterglow ?
  Where 'mid red woods the maples sit,

Like scarlet-mantled sagamores,
Who, from their totemed wigwam doors,
   Watch through red fires the ghost-dance flit.

At night, as comes the fox, shall come
The spirit of the frost, whose thumb
   Shall squeeze the chestnut burs, and press
Each husk bare ; whisper every flower
Such tales of death that in an hour
   It dies of utter happiness.

Until the moon sets I shall walk,
And listen wold and woodland talk
   Of by-gone lovely nights and days :
My soul—made silent intimate
Of all its sorrow—soon and late
   A neighbor of the autumn haze.

XIII.

What revelations fill with song
The cycles ? and to what belong
   Life's far convictions of the light ?
Through which the spirit waxeth strong,

The darkling soul surmounts the night
By builded rainbows to some height,
Near mountain stars of Truth and Right,
Beyond the vulture wing of Wrong ?—

Nature ! who still adjusts the deeps
Of her soul's needs to man's ; and keeps
Such grave response as grief shall hear
When on her heart it sinks and weeps ;
For every gladness, clean and clear
Its glad reflection lying near—
The wild accord of hope and fear
Which in her inmost bosom sleeps.

XIV.

The mallow, like an Elfland moon,
Within the marsh gleams grottoed gold ;
Its bell-shaped blossom seems to hold
All the lost beauty of last June :
September's mist haunts, white and cold,
The windings of the forest stream,
As death might haunt soft eyes that dream.

And who with idle words hath stood,
   With idle thoughts, and gazed into
   The face of one he loved and knew,
Dying in all her womanhood ?
   No words, but silence, then will do,
When the belovèd falls asleep,
No thoughts but help the heart to weep.

XV.

The snowy flutter of a hand
   Shall glitter in the morning mist,
   And from the mist a jewelled wrist
Of dew shall beckon and command :
And hope shall see the unknown Land
   Of Far Away beyond the Dawn,
   Where, crowned with roses wild and wan,
The Futures of the World speed on.

Along the eve a fiery arm
   Shall point us to the waning west,
   And all the sorrow, that oppressed
The heart once, shall become a charm

2

Of patience, which shall so transform
  The Present in the Long Ago,
  The Past—from lands we used to know—
Shall lean with lilies dropping slow.

XVI.

Pearl-lilac blent with pearly rose,
  The dawn bloomed slowly out of dusk,—
  As some huge cactus from its husk
Might burst a bloom whose chalice glows
  A grotto of transmuted dyes ;—
Such wild, auroral light as flows
  On ice-peaks from unearthly skies.

Dove-purple shifting into shades
  Of opal,—like the tints which dwell
  With fire in the ocean-shell,—
The sunset flashed above the glades
  Through skies of nacre and of flame ;—
Such supernatural light as braids
  Dim coral caves that have no name.

XVII.

Draw from thine eyes the veil which hides
　　Ideal vision's beckonings ;
Behold the beauty which abides
　　Beneath the common-place of things :
No brook within the woodland then
　　But shows its sparkling god to thee ;
　　Upon the ancient hills no tree
　　Whose whispering spirit thou shalt not see,
Fairer than children born of men.

Refine thy flesh, which never hears
　　The inner music of all things,—
The deaf flesh,—from thy spirit's ears,
　　And list the vaster voice that sings
With pregnant lips unto the Earth :
　　Mornings, who shout from sky to sky
　　God's psalms to which the eves reply—
　　The everlasting heavens that cry
The visible truths of death and birth.

XVIII.

The flowers of the fall I seek :
  The golden aster,—like a gauze
  Of gold,—beneath the nodding haws,
Or making gay each tangled creek ;
The hairy, small herb-Robert, lost,—
  Yet seen,—among the weeds which crush
  Or crowd it, with its bluish blush ;
Its rough, low stalk stung red with frost.

Around the rail-fence, climbing up,
  The nightshade hangs rich berries down,—
  Clusters of cochineal,—that drown
The flowering bind-weed's pendant cup :
And where the boggy bottom sets
  Its burs as breastworks and as tents,
  Like bivouacking regiments,
The cat-tails lift their bayonets.

From amaranth—in tree and flower—
  To asphodel—in weed and bloom—
  The season swings a magic loom

Of sun and mist from hour to hour :
In its wide warp it weaves the dyes
   Of morning's brilliant blue and gray ;
   And crimson through the weft of day
Flings the wild woof of evening skies.

XIX.

What intimations made them wise,
   The mournful pine, the mighty beech ?
   Some strange and esoteric speech—
(Communicated from the skies
In secret symbols)—that invokes
   The boles which sleep within the seeds,
   And out of narrow darkness leads
The vast assemblies of the oaks.

Within his knowledge what one reads
   The poems written by the flowers?
   The sermons, past all speech that 's ours,
Preached in the gospel of the weeds ?—
Thou eloquence of coloring !

Oh, thoughts of syllabled perfume !
Oh, beauty uttered into bloom !
Thou utterance named blossoming !

XX.

What time the great lobelia fills
   The wildwood with young hopes of spring—
And bluets, scattered o'er the hills,
     Bloom, starry-sown, through everything—
     My fancy takes me wandering,
Looking from wizard window-sills.

In lavender lights, which sleep among
   The ferns, my heart is at a loss
To know the love that leads along
     Down magic ways of faëry moss—
     A brook, perhaps, will call across,
An unseen bluebird burst in song.

And so to reach the land, which lies
   Yon side the world, we just can see ;
Wherein the Elfland cities rise,

Faint haunts of musk and melody ;
Wherein the singing-bird and bee,
And congregated flowers grow wise.

XXI.

Upon the Earth what hints are rife
   Of life when change hath left us still !
   When death within the flesh doth kill
All recollection that was life !
   What hints, which tell us not alone
Immortal is the spirit, for
Flesh too,—corruption can but mar,—
   The incorruptible puts on :

The blood shall fill a part that 's higher
   Of color, and pervade all flowers ;
   The brain inform the twinkling hours
With dreams of resurrected fire ;
   The heart perform the function of
A fragrance ; and the countenance
Lend new expression to, perchance,
   The face of beauty that we love.

XXII.

Oh, joy, to walk the way which goes
　　Through woods of sweet-gum and of beech !
　　Where, like a ruby left in reach,
The berry of the dog-wood glows :
　　Or where the bristling hillsides mass,
　　'Twixt belts of tawny sassafras,
Brown shocks of corn in wigwam rows !

Where, in the hazy morning, runs
　　The stony branch that pools and drips,
　　The red-haws and the wild-rose hips
Are strewn like pebbles ; and the sun's
　　Own gold seems captured by the weeds ;
　　To see, through scintillating seeds,
The hunters steal with glimmering guns !

Oh, joy, to go the path which lies
　　Through woodlands where the oaks are tall !
　　Beneath the misty moon of fall,
Whose ghostly girdle prophesies
　　A morn wind-swept and gray with rain ;

When, o'er the lonely, leafy lane,
The night-bird, like a dead leaf, flies !

To stand within the dewy ring
    Where pale death smites the boneset blooms,
    And everlasting's flowers, and plumes
Of mint, with aromatic wing !
    And hear the creek,—whose sobbing seems
    A wild-man murmuring in his dreams,—
And insect violins that sing !

Or where the dim persimmon-tree
    Wastes on the path its frosty fruit,
    And in its top the owl doth hoot
Beneath the moon and mist, to see
    The outcast Year come,—Hagar-wise,—
    With far-off, melancholy eyes,
And lips that thirst for sympathy !

XXIII.

Along my mind flies suddenly
    A wildwood thought that will not die,

That makes me brother to the bee,
   And kindred to the butterfly :
A thought, such as gives perfume to
   The blushes of the bramble-rose,
   And, fixed in quivering crystal, glows
A captive in the prismed dew.

It leads the feet no certain way,
   No frequent path of human feet ;
Its wild eyes follow me all day,
   All day I hear its wild heart beat :
And in the night it sings and sighs
   The songs the winds and waters love ;
   Its wild heart lying tranced above,
And tranced the wildness of its eyes.

XXIV.

With eyes regardless of their tears
   I look upon the twilight fields :
   The stars swing down their shimmering shields,
And fill the phalanx of their spears.
I can not see, I only know

A flower dies beneath my feet ;
The fragrance of its death is sweet
And bitter as my heart's own woe.

With thoughts which find not what they seek
I question Earth and Heaven, and find
That they are dark and I am blind,
And in my blindness very weak.
I do not know, I only feel
Behind all death a purpose stands,   `
With hallowed and magnetic hands,
Beneficent and strong to heal.

XXV.

These too shall tell me what my heart,
And what my soul desireth :—
The flowers, that bloom serene for death,
The stars, that know no mortal part.
One shall inspire my heart with acts
Of life so that the death responds ;
One to the soul breathe higher facts
Of death that shall annul such bonds.

Sufficient for my love these terms,
  Beyond my understanding's scope :
  I merely know all life must grope
Not downward from its darkling germs.
Sufficient for my faith is such :
  That, in the narrow night which binds
The seed, its life shall feel in touch
  With light above it seeks and finds.

XXVI.

Beyond the violet-colored hill
The golden-deepened daffodil
Of dusk bloomed out with thrill on thrill :
And, drifting west, the crescent moon
Gleamed like a sword of Scanderoon
A satrap dropped on floors of gold ;
Near which,—one loosened gem that rolled
Out of the jewelled scimitar,—
      The evening star.

Behind the trees, where, darkly deep
As indigo, the shadows sleep,—

As if the Titan world would heap
A throne with purple for its god,
Whose pomp comes with vermilion shod,—
The west, 'thwart which the wild-ducks fly,
Burns, richer than the orient dye
Phœnician vessels brought from Tyre,
   With carmine fire.

Above black hills the heavens are gray.
The sear, bleak forests sound and sway.
The ashen rain-clouds roll this way.
The green grig in the withered weeds
Sings, and the wild snipe seeks the reeds.
With hurling winds,—that moan and wail
Like Demon-huntsmen,—dark with hail
And rain, which blots the cabin's light,
   Comes on the night.

XXVII.

There is a rushing in the woods,
The murmur-haunted solitudes,
 When night comes in with winds that sweep

The wild rain from the hills ; and reap
The roaring harvest of the leaves
With sounding scythes Death stalks behind
And Desolation, fierce and blind,
Heaping the storm's tumultuous sheaves.

There is a sighing in the woods,
The rocks of hill-topped solitudes,
When on the night, the winds have strewn
With crowding clouds, the stormy moon
Bursts like a herald shouting *Cease !*
Through darkness o'er a battle-field
Of Hell ; the splendor of his shield
Inscribed with silence and with peace.

XXVIII.

The storm,—that makes the sky its own,
And smites its spirit through Earth's nerves,
And, like an instrument which serves
High purposes to us unknown
Of song which knows not that it sings,—
Itself is all majestic things

Imagination forms or feels ;
Itself all wonders it reveals
   To thought, which knows but semblances
   Of such concealed realities.

       .

The star, that flames through storm and crowds
   An instant with its utterance
   Of silence and serene romance,
And glides again into the clouds,
   Shone for some present end, and filled
   A moment's need as Heaven willed :—
A thought, some dreamer labored for,
Immaculate as is a star ;
   A hope, some weary watcher read
   Pale in the loved face of his dead.

XXIX.

Towards evening, where the sweet-gum flung
   Its thorny balls among the weeds,
   And where the milkweed's sleepy seeds,—
A fairy Feast of Lanterns,—swung ;
   The crickets tuned a plaintive lyre,

LIBRARY OF THE UNIVERSITY OF CALIFORNIA

And o'er the hills the sunset hung
  A purple parchment scrawled with fire.

From silver-blue to amethyst
  The shadows broadened in the vale ;
  And, belt by belt, the pearly pale
Aladdin fabric of the mist
  Stretched its vague exhalation far ;
A jewel on an Afrit's wrist,
  One star scarred sunset's cinnabar.

Then night drew near, as when, alone,
  The heart and soul grow intimate ;
  And on the hills the twilight sate
With shadows, whose wild robes were sown
  With dreams and whispers—dreams, that led
The heart once with love's monotone,
  Searching among the living dead.

XXX.

Of Life and of Eternity
These are the dreams which came to me :
The one :—A whitened whirl of sea ;

A gallows beetling through the rains,
And, tossing in its rusty chains,
A skeleton on the gallows-tree :
Gaunt ravens roost above or tear
Long strips from shrivelled skin and hair :
A ship hurls pounding on the rocks : ·
Wild minute-guns boom through the spume
And crashing surf : out of the gloom
The strangled dead leers down and mocks.

An incorporeal solitude
Which darkness out of darkness hewed,
The other dream : enormous deeps
Of naught, where ancient Silence sleeps,
The eldest of Heav'n's Titan brood :—
In unilluminated night,
Vast and insufferable white
A summit soars : its light, which dyes
Not darkness, of itself is born :
Around its splendor, as in scorn,
Night's dark, defiant radiance lies.

3

XXXI.

Past midnight, gathering from the west,
  With rolling rain the storm came on,
  And tore and tossed until the dawn,
Like some dark demon of unrest :
  The   stairways   creaked ;   the   chimneys
    boomed ;
I heard the wild leaves blown about
The windy windows ; and the shout
  Of forests that the storm had doomed.

I listened, and remembered how
  On yesterday I went alone
  A sunlit path through fields o'ergrown
With sumach brakes, turned crimson now ;
  Where asters strung blue pearls and white
Beside the golden-rod's soft ruff ;
The groundsel, silvery puff on puff,
  Danced many a twinkling witch's-light.

Her joy the Autumn uttered so
  To skies where gold and azure blent ;

Now storm is the embodiment
Of all her utterance of woe :
The two within me so decide
That of the two my mind partakes,—
As one, who walks asleep, awakes,
Walks on and thinks, " To·night I died.

XXXII.

What sympathies of Heaven and Earth
The human *ego* enters in !
The universal stain of sin
Which qualifies this from its birth
Denying it their highest worth.
There is a parallel of kin
'Twixt earth and man, that dignifies
Endeavor with such sympathies.

The all mysterious wisdom waits
In mountain, wood and waterfall,
Sky, rock and sea, to hear the call
Of something—firmer than the Fates—
Deep in the soul it elevates ;

And to the splendor of the All
Advances, through the night's immense,
The spirit of experience.

So think I now while, long and loud,
   The wind its maniac music beats,
   And storm a madman's song repeats
To echoes in the rushing cloud ;
While all the world to wrath is vowed,
   No starlight triumphs or defeats
The darkness and the rain that raves
Above the all-unheeding graves.

XXXIII.

All night the rain-gusts shook the leaves
   Around my window ; and the blast
   Rumbled the flickering flue, and fast
The storm streamed from the dripping eaves.
As if—'neath skies gone mad with fear—
   The witches' sabboth galloped past,
The forests leapt like startled deer.

All night I heard the sweeping sleet ;
  And when the morning came, as slow
  As pale affliction, with the woe
Of all the world dragged at her feet,
No spear of purple shattered through
  The dark gray of the east ; no bow,
Whose golden arrows cleft the blue.

But rain, that whipped the windows ; filled
  The spouts with rushing ; and around
  The garden stamped, and sowed the ground
With limbs and leaves ; the wood-pool filled
With overgurgling.—Bleak and cold
  The fields looked, where the foot-path wound
Through teasel and bur-marigold. . . .

There is a kindness in such days
  Of gloom, that doth console regret
  With sympathy of tears which wet
Old eyes that watch the back-log blaze—
A kindness, alien to the deep
  Glad blue of sunny days that let
No thought in of the sad who weep.

XXXIV.

This dawn, through which the Autumn glowers,—
  As might a face within our sleep,
  With coffined eyes that can not weep,
And dead brows bound with withered flowers,—
Is sunset to some sister land ;
  A land of ruins and of palms ;
  Rich sunset, crimson with long calms,—
  Whose burning belt low mountains bar,—
That sees some brown Rebecca stand
Beside a well the camel band
  Winds down to 'neath the evening-star.

O sunset, sister to this dawn !
  O dawn, whose face is turned away !
  Who gazest not upon this day
But back upon the day that's gone !
Enamoured so of loveliness,
  The retrospect of what thou wast,
  Oh, to thyself the present trust !
  And as thy past make beautiful

With hues, that never can grow less !
Waiting thy pleasure to express
New beauty, lest the world grow dull !

XXXV.

At day-break from the woodland come
 Echoes of hunting ; or the chop
  Of some far woodman's axe, that cleaves
  The tingling oak, whose russet leaves
 Drop drowsy where the white chips drop :
The air is fragrant with the loam,
 Where, through the mists of steaming gold,
 The sudden sun strikes fold on fold.

Out of the window, filmed with fog,
 I look into the wreck which was
  The kitchen-garden, drenched with rain ;
  Among the death I mark again
 One pink convolvulus—that draws
A gray vignette along a log,—
 With pencilled tendrils washed and wan—
 The garden-legend's colophon.

XXXVI.

More storm than calm, less gold than gray,
    Along the years our lives must tread,
Makes sad the scenes around our way,
    Makes grave the heavens overhead :
      For on Life's storied page, behold,
    Reflections of Earth's countless dead !
The neutral tint Time's fingers lay
    Around a tale that 's never told.

Time writes with sunshine less than rain,
    With starlight less than mist, the scroll—
A thousand memories of pain
    To one of joy—of his own soul :
      The golden hues of life occur
    In his dim palimpsest, whose whole
Death scrawls with dusty lines again,
    Making the scroll one leaden blur.

XXXVII.

Down in the woods a sorcerer,
    Out of rank rain and death, distills,

Through chill alembics of the air,
Aromas that brood everywhere
  Among the dingles of the hills :
  The bitter myrrh of dead leaves fills
Wet valleys, where the gaunt weeds bleach,
  With dreamy scents of wood decay ;—
  As if a spirit all the day
Sat breathing softly 'neath the beech.

What other eyes shall see her flit,
  The white witch of the wild perfumes,
Among her sleepy owls, that sit,
A fluffy white, in crescent-lit
  Lost glens and opalescent glooms ?
  Where for her magic buds and blooms
Mysterious perfumes, while she stands,
  A fragrant radiance, summoning
  The eery odors that take wing,
Like bubbles, from her dewy hands.

XXXVIII.

With leagues of fog, which showed the sun
  An agate-red without a ray,

And drowned the world in ghostly gray,
The chill, autumnal day begun :
A phantom in the mist, a run
    Foamed over phantom ledges lone
    Of forest that seemed far away,
        A forest of enchanted stone.

With horses saffron to the knees
    A country cart drove through the fog ;
    Its creaking wheels grown one great clog
Of clay, and clanking swingle-trees ;
Its smothered rumble did not cease
    Till hidden in the woodland mist,
    Where, leaning on his axe and log,
        The muffled woodman blew his fist.

Another world I wander in
    Of unlaid ghosts and dreams unfled ;
    A twilight world of drowsyhead
And mystery, built figment-thin
Between the worlds of death and sin ;
        Where dim and vague and incomplete

And substance less seem things not dead,
  And sorrowful as sadly sweet.

XXXIX.

Among the woods they call to me—
  The lights that lie on rock and stream ;
Chaste voices of such ecstasy
  As walks with hushed lips through a dream :
They stand in nimbused essences,
  Or flash with glittering limbs across
  Their golden shadows on the moss,
Or slip in silver through the trees.

What love can give the heart in me
  More hope and exaltation than
The hand of light that tips the tree
  And calls me from the world of man ?
That reaches foamy fingers through
  The broken ripple, and denies
  No sparkling speech of fearless eyes,
Nor lips that sing and still pursue ?

XL.

Oh, bright the day, and calm and cool
With clouds, like cotton-fields that swoon
Beneath the silver summer moon ;
And, quiet as a forest pool,
Where Autumn stoops to comb her locks,
And strews with rainbow leaves and roon,
The shadows rest among the rocks.

The sun pours airy amber on
The withered wood-ways, where the late
Green-crickets' oboes vibrate ;
And, fainter than the lines of dawn,
The fields shine labyrinthed with rays,
With gossamers, that figurate
Bright figments of the feverish days.

Beyond the yarrow's meekness now,
Wood-sorrel's lowliness, the shy
Hepatica's humility,
The Year hath grown : makes brave her brow

With crowning crimson of the lands,
  And robes her limbs in sunset dye,
And by the lonely waters stands.

XLI.

Pure thought-creations of the mind,
  Within the circle of the soul,—
  The emanations that control
  Life to its God-predestined goal,—
Are spirit shapes no flesh can bind :
  Within the soul desire ordains
  Achievements which the will obtains ;
And far above us, on before,
Our thoughts—a beautiful people—soar,
  To wait us on celestial plains.

So Nature pours her thoughts in forms—
  Realities we move among—
  Of fragrance, color, and of song ;
  Sense-emanations which belong,
Invisible, to spiritual charms ;
  The sensuous substance of her thought

From immaterial matter wrought—
Matter, which death can not annul,
That constitutes the Beautiful,
    And dead, repeats itself from naught.

XLII.

Give me the streams ! which counterfeit
    The starlight of autumnal skies ;
The silent, shadowy waters, lit
    With fire like a woman's eyes :
Slow waters which, in autumn, glass
The scarlet-strewn and golden grass,
    And drink the sunset's tawny dyes.

Give me the pools ! which lie among
    The centuried forests : give me those
Deep, dim, and sad as shadows hung
    Dark 'neath the sunset's sombre rose ;
Pale pools, in whose vague mirrors look—
Like ragged gypsies round a book
    Of magic—trees in wild repose.

No quiet thing or innocent
   Of water, earth, or air shall please
My soul now : but the violent
   Between the sunset and the trees :
The fierce, the splendid and intense,
That love matures in innocence,
   Like awful music, give me these.

XLIII.

As Nature in herself resolves
   All parts of beauty to one whole,
And from the perfect whole evolves
   The high ideas that control
Advancement, till the time be ripe
To doff disguise and, type by type,
   Reveal the emanated soul :

So should the Beautiful in man
   Evolve the best in him ; to be
The lofty purpose life began
   For ends which only Heaven shall see—

The absolute, that sees how thought
Its high ideal's shape hath wrought
  To be its far affinity.

XLIV.

I hold them here ; they are no less ;
  I see them still—the changeful grays
  Of threatening skies above the haze—
    My hills ! that roll long, murmuring miles
Of savage-painted wilderness,
    On which the saddened sunlight smiles ;
  Or, like a fallen-angel's frown—
  Severe beneath a burning crown—
Through sombre silvers, that oppress
  With clouds its glory, rushes down.

I hear the coming storm again ;
  Again behold the streaming clouds ;
  The autumn wind drives down and crowds
    Wild, sibylline voices through the leaves,
And whispering octaves of the rain ;
    A wilder wind, vibrating, heaves

God's music through the rolling woods—
Upon my soul the grandeur broods
Like some archangel's trumpet strain,
  Or organ-pomp that sweeps all moods.

XLV.

Such circumstance of passionate praise
  Hath no religion ; and the creeds
No pomp of worship or of grace
Like Nature's, standing face to face
  With God, whose inmost thought she reads :
  No multitude of words she needs,
Since all her worship is one word
Of love, like that creation heard.

God leaves progression in her care :
  Through her it must materialize—
Our mother ! with strong lips of prayer,
Majestic-browed, with hands that bare
  Immortal fire from the skies :
  Who looks with no evasive eyes
Through life, and, smiling, sees beneath
The beautiful, dark eyes of death.

XLVI.

Between the sunset and the stars
   Long clouds lie—as the sachems loom,
   In war-paint and the eagle plume,
Among their wampumed warriors,
When council fires burn red and set
   On stoic cheeks the battle bloom,
Around the smoking calumet.

Beneath the stars and hunter's-moon
   The frost spreads ghosts of pearls, that glance
   Like goblin jewels in the dance
Which whirls on fairied hills of June :
The night is calm ; no luminous veil
   Conceals the spirit utterance
Of her dark beauty, pure and pale.

XLVII.

I sat alone with song and sleep,
   And in the singing silence heard
The darkness draw from out the deep,

With star on star, like word on word :
A sound of twilight and swift shades
Materializing into Night,
Who hears the breaking waves of light,
And towards the shores of Morning wades.

I sat alone with dawn and death,
　And in my waking vision saw
The form of silence, like a breath
　Of bodiless beauty and of awe,
Whose sibyl eyes said unto me
　The things the sealed lips would not word,
　That eons of the stars record
In volumes of eternity.

XLVIII.

The dead gold of the marybud,
　The dusky, tarnished orange-red
　Of zinnias, fire the flower-bed,
Like frosty autumn gleams that scud
　The darkening dusks and gradual dawns
　Above the mist-enveloped lawns.

With tired eyes, and heart grown grave,
  And thoughts more listless than the night,
  I watch the dwindling of the light,
And hear the rising night-winds rave,
  As one might hear, when half-asleep,
  Another self make moan and weep.

XLIX.

Behold, the winds have speech and speak !
  The stars of heaven are eloquent !
A voice within us bids us seek
  The word the flowers write with scent :
  The spiritual encouragement
Of beauty that the burning scrolls
Of eve and morning give our souls.

There is one language of the mart ;
  Another of the rocks and trees :
Unrest and greed is this one's heart ;
  The heart of that is rest and peace :
  Within our souls we know of these ;

They lead us by the myths we love,
Yet never see and know not of.

L.

When thorn-tree copses still were bare
  And black along the brawling brook;
  When catkined willows blurred and shook
Great tawny tangles in the air;
  In bottom-lands, the first thaw makes
An oozy bog, beneath the trees,
  Prophetic of the spring that wakes,
Sang the sonorous Hylodes.

Now when wild winds have stripped the thorn,
  And strewn with leaves the forest creek;
  Now when the woods look brown and bleak,
And webs are frosty white at morn;
  At night beneath the spectral sky,
A far foreboding cry I hear—
  The wild-fowl calling as they fly?
Or vague voice of the dying year?

LI.

Night,—who within heaven's uttermost
   Dark walls uncloses shadowy gates,—
   Beyond the Spirit of Light she hates,
Speeds like a ghost before a ghost
Upon the twilight-haunted coast
   Of death between the seas of sleep :
Her lips are dumb with awe that hears ;
   And in her eyes, that never weep,
Is anguish of eternal tears.

Out of the terrible gulfs of God
   Into God's awful deeps she goes,
   Revealing in heaven's golden glows
The ways her footsteps tread and trod
From period to period :
   Her lips are still—for she hath heard
God's voice that moves the universe :
   Her eyes are sad beyond the word—
The eyes of vastness gazed in hers.

LII.

And still to hold the heart at tryst
  When chestnuts hiss among the coals,
  The hallowed evening near All Souls,
When all the night is moon and mist,
  And all the world is mystery.
To dream lips kissed—that death hath kissed;
  Eyes seen—no eyes can ever see ;
  And love returned—long lost to thee !

To hear the weird wind's velvet glove
  Flutter the window : or the knob
  Of some dark door turn, with a sob
As when love comes to murder love
  And steals with horror through the room :
Or now the iron gauntlet of
  The gust—a knight, who comes with gloom
  To meet his lady by her tomb.

So fancy takes the mind, and paints
  The darkness with eidolon light,

And writes the dead's romance in white,
On the dim Evening of All Saints :
　　Unheard the hissing nuts ; the clink
Of falling coals, whose shadow faints,—
　　A spectre risen on memory's brink,—
Around us where we sit and think.

LIII.

No thing occult of Heaven or Earth,
　　Or influence of such, I feel
But hath a meaning and a worth
　　God in His wisdom doth conceal :
Reflections of another birth,
　　Existent with and kin to ours,
　　Announcing through supernal powers
Facts of a world it would reveal.

In Nature dost perceive it, too,
　　This other life thou canst not see :—
A spirit sparkles in the dew,
　　The trees have tongues which speak to thee :
That Earth is green and Heaven, blue,

The sight alone may satisfy ;
The soul sees with a different eye
The meaning 'neath the mystery.

LIV.

The shadow of uncertain things
And all unearthly whisperings,—
 The premonition pale of blight,—
 Leans from the sepulchre of night ;
And on the Earth fall shadowings,
  And prophesies of near decay ;
 And, lovelier than a dead delight,
  The starlit skies of glittering gray.

Still shall the Season claim and keep
Her wild-girl beauty ; doubly deep
 The purport of her dreams shall rise
 Out of her heart into her eyes,
Till very dreaming makes her sleep ;
  And death, with pale, pure lips and arms,
 Shall touch her from the frosty skies,
  Making a memory of her charms.

LV.

Sometime shall Beauty hide no more
   The chaste conceptions she conceives
   Beneath the abstract veil she weaves
Before her face the few adore ;
   The self-denying few, who long
   Live lofty lives of art and song,
And, dying, leave the world less poor.

No more are these alone when she,
   From the subjective world she rules,
   Confronts the falsehood of the schools
With her high front of purity ;
   And on the dark and general way
   Lets fall her individual ray
That low as well as high may see.

LVI.

The ghost of what was loveliness
   Sits in the waning woods, with bare
   And bleeding feet, and wintry hair,

And brows the thorns of care distress ;
  She makes a comfort of despair,
And, Rachel-like, with eyes wept red,
Refuses to be comforted.

To funeral torches for the Year,
  With tree by tree, the forests turned ;
  Then, fiery coals in ashes, burned
A few last leaves among the sere ;
  Where, robed with purple pomp, she yearned
To die, like some fair queen ; and died,
Crowned with magnificence and pride.

LVII.

She meets us with impressive hands
  And eyes of earnest emphasis
Between the known and unknown lands,
  And beautifies us with her kiss,
This spirit of the solitude
Named Meditation ; thought-imbued,
  On whom all beauty ministers ;

Whose silent, dreaming worshippers
Lay unresisting hands in hers,
Knowing their hearts are understood.

The holy harp she holds and smites
    Was tuned among concordant spheres ;
The heavenly pen with which she writes
    Was dipped in angel smiles and tears :
Between her eyebrows and her eyes
The starry stamp of silence lies ;
    Between her symboled lips and tongue,
    The song the stars of morning sung :
    To *this* her heavenly harp is strung,
In *that* her holy pen is wise.

LVIII.

Again the night is wild with rain ;
    Again distracted with the gale ;
    Upon the hills I hear a wail
Of lamentation and of pain,
    As when, on some high burial-place,

Moaning among the windy graves,
The Indian squaws lament the braves,
  Who fell in battle for their race.

Another day of storm shall dawn
  Within the east ; and, darkly lit,
  Its brows of stern abstraction knit,
Absorbed in moody thought, pass on.—
  Bear not too hard, is all I ask,
Upon the hearts that toil and yearn !
O despotism of days, that spurn
  All gladness, with your frowning mask !

LIX.

No wind is this which cries forlorn
  Around the hilltops and the woods !—
  Earth, weary with her multitudes
Of dead, despairing of the morn,
  Calls through illimitable night
The wailing words no thing may know :
  Deep in her memory-haunted sight

Sleeps no remembrance of delight,
But death and everlasting woe.

No wind ! a voice whose sense is form ;
    A form whose sense is but a sound ;
    That smites the constant skies around,
And shakes the steadfast hills with storm :
    Along life's desolate deep it cries
The words death's sterile lips must learn
    From Law, the Law that never dies—
    Such utterless wild speech as sighs
In stone and cinerary urn.

LX.

I heard the wind, before the morn
    Stretched gaunt, gray fingers at my pane,
    Drive clouds down, a dark dragon train ;
Its iron visor closed, a horn
    Of steel from out the north it wound.—
No morn like yesterday's ! whose mouth,
A cool carnation, from the south

Breathed through a golden reed the sound
Of days that drop sweet gold upon
Melodious silver floors of dawn.

And all of yesterday is lost
    And swallowed in to-day's wild light—
    The birth deformed of day and night,
The illegitimate, who cost
    Its mother secret tears and sighs ;
Unlovely since unloved ; and chilled
With sorrows and the shame that filled
    Its parents' love ; which was not wise
In passion as that day and night
Who love, and marry light to light.

LXI.

We know not of one mood that 's hers,
    Or glad or grave, which hath not drawn
Its source from God's blue universe,
    As th' hours draw the day from dawn—
Nature's ! who holds us quietly

But earnestly, as by a spell,
Whose contact with us seems to be
    Actual and yet intangible.

In us she thus asserts her claims
    Of kinship and divine control ;
God-teacher of exalted aims,
    The high consents of star and soul :
Imperfectly man sees and feels,
    Through earthly mediums of his fate,
The premonitions she reveals
    For issues that shall elevate.

LXII.

Down through the dark, indignant trees,
    On indistinguishable wings
    Of storm, the wind of evening swings ;
Before its insane anger flees
    The mad leaf and the broken bough :
There is a rushing, as when seas
    Of thunder beat an iron prow

On reefs of wrath and roaring wreck :
'Mid stormy leaves, a hurrying speck
Of flickering blackness, driven by
The mad bats whirl along the sky.

Part of the sadness of such eves,
 A melancholy—visible
 Within the forest's wizard spell—
A gaunt girl stands among the leaves,
 The night-wind in her dolorous dress :
Symbolic of the life that grieves,
 The toil that patience makes not less,
Her load of fallen faggots there.
A wilder shadow sweeps the air ;
She hears the bleak, bewildered hum
Of woods, and waits, like grief struck dumb.

LXIII.

No songs but what are sorrowful
 And sweet in pensive notes and words,
 Shall fill my heart, as singing birds
Might build a nest within a skull. . . .

The nunlike days, in stoles of white,
  Chant requiems for the dying Year ;
  The monklike nights about her bier,
  In cowls of black, with lights that blear,
The service for the dead recite.

Into my soul the litanies
  Of life and death strike golden bars ;
  I hear the far, responding stars,
That voice the multiplying skies,
Reverberate from cause to cause
  Results that terminate in man ;
  From world to world, the rounding plan
  Of change, that circumstance began,
Of which both life and death are laws.

LXIV.

'No sunlight strews with gold the plain ;
  No moonlight stains the hill with white ;
Clouds, sullen with the undropped rain,
  And motionless with unspent spite,
Dome deep with uninvaded gray

The dull, ignoble term of day,
　　The duller ultimate of night.

Yea, ev'n the mad, marauding Wind,
　　Who whipped his wild steeds east and west,
Whose whirlwind wheels rolled down and dinned
　　Along the booming forest's crest,
Lies dead upon his mountains, where
　　His sister Breezes beat the breast,
Sighing through their unshaken hair.

LXV.

The griefs of Nature like her joys
　　Are placid and yet passionate ;
　　These, in her heart which knows no hate,
She for the beautiful employs.　.　.　.
Behold how thoughts of happiness
Rebuke the tears on sorrow's face !
Upon the brow of joy no less
How grief restrains with seriousness !
Each to the other lending grace.

Oh, tenderness of grief that knows
 Some happiness still lies before !
 That for the rose which blooms no more
Shall bloom a no less perfect rose !
Oh, pensiveness of joy that takes
 Sweet dignity from grief that died !
Remembering, though the morning shakes
Her bright locks from blue eyes and wakes,
 Night sleeps on the same mountain side !

LXVI.

What sorcery do the woods conceal
 Desired by the desperate days ?
 With feet of fog and hands of haze
They search the crumbled woods and steal
With mutt'rings,—gaunt as hags who deal
 In witchcraft,—where the dark bough sways,
And, venerable, with staff a-slant,
Death sits like some old mendicant.

Around me all 's despondency,
 Like darkness on th' unwilling world ;

A twilight sadness held and hurled
With sobbing silence over me :
I feel the thorns no man shall see,
    The snake which strikes where none is curled—
Oh, melancholy of the soul
That struggles and attains no goal !

———

The song-birds ? are they flown away ?
    The song-birds of the summer-time,
That sang their souls into the day,
    And set the laughing days to rhyme ?—
No catbird scatters through the hush
    The sparkling crystals of its song ;
Within the woods no hermit-thrush
    Trails an enchanted flute along,
A sweet assertion of the hush.

All day the crows fly cawing past ;
    The acorns drop ; the forests scowl :
At night I hear the bitter blast
    Hoot with the hooting of the owl.
The wild creeks freeze ; the ways are strewn

With leaves that rot : beneath the tree
The bird, that set its toil to tune,
　And made a home for melody,
Lies dead beneath the death-white moon.

KNOWLEDGE AND BEAUTY.

SHALL I forget and yet behold
How earth hath said its secret, to
The violet's appealing blue,
Of fragrance ; old as earth is old,
The knowledge that is never told ?

Shall I behold and yet forget,
The soft blue of the heaven fell,
Between the dusk and dawn, to tell
Its purpose, to the violet,
Of beauty none hath fathomed yet ?

Between the earth and sky, above,
The wind goes singing all day long ;
And he who listens to its song
May catch an instant's meaning of
The end of life, the end of love.

ELEUSINIAN.

PRAXITELEAN marbles, fairer forms
   Than Phryne's and than hers, who loved
   and knew
The Attic cynic's soul, the rosy charms
  Of lovely Laïs, gradually grew
Before my eyelids, like a floating mist,
Out of the music of the citharist.

And there were Dryads, laughing sidewise eyes,
   Among Cithæron's ash-trees ; and uncouth
Brown Satyrs, dancing 'neath Bœotian skies ;
   And by a fountain sat a beautiful youth,
Like some white flow'r, with dim, dejected grace,
In love with the reflection of his face.

And then a chord of soft bewitchment swept
   Along my soul ; and, oh ! within a vale,
Like some young god, a godlike mortal slept ;

And there was splendor on the heights, and pale
The presence of supernal purity,
Whose face was as a marble melody.

And now two chords, that were two hands that
    strewed
  Innumerable memories upon
My eyelids—and my spirit understood
  How, ages past, I was Endymion ;
Feeling once more the old, wild rapture of
Immortal sorrow and immortal love.

CHRYSELEPHANTINE.

1.

AMONG the hills and morning-colored ways
Let us go forth, oh, let us go with singing !
Within the hearts of better bosoms bringing
A gift of gifts, one day of all our days,
Unto the golden temple of God's praise,
And ivory altar of the beautiful :
The woods are deep, the woods are dark and cool ;
Let us go forth with timbrels of rejoicing,
And lutes of love, and lips forever voicing
The beautiful !

2.

The milkwort's pink and barley's gold and green,
Twined with the purple of the wilding pansies,
Wild pansies—dreamy as an old romance is
With sad blue eyes of some enchanted queen

In fairyland, through fable casements seen—
Wreathed with mauve leaves, to give to loveliness,
On moss as cool and soft as a caress :
 Let us go forth, arrayed as is the morning,
 With psalteries of praise, to the adorning
  Of loveliness !

3.

No spotted snake shall hiss within the shrine
 High God ordains, within the heav'nlit distance,
 Young love shall build, with life to give as-
  sistance,
Of fragrance and of song; whereon shall shine
All of His stars to make it all divine :
No toad without shall croak ; but purity
Shall guard the entrance,—none impure shall
  see !—
 For worshippers of beauty in the spirit,
 The offerers of thought, which doth inherit
  But purity.

SIBYLLINE.

I.

THERE is a glory in the apple boughs
   Of silver moonlight ; like a torch of myrrh,
Burning upon an altar of sweet vows,
   Dropped from the hand of some wan worshipper :
And there is life among the apple blooms
   Of whisp'ring winds ; as if a god addressed
The flamen from the sanctuary glooms
    With secrets of the bourne that hope hath
      guessed,
Saying : "Behold ! a darkness which illumes,
     A waking which is rest."

2.

There is a blackness in the apple trees
   Of tempest ; like the ashes of an urn

Hurt hands have gathered upon blistered knees,
  With salt of tears, out of the flames that burn :
And there is death among the blooms, that fill
  The night with breathless scent,—as when, above
The priest, the vision of his faith doth will
  Forth from his soul the beautiful form thereof,—
Saying :   "Behold ! a silence never still ;
    The other form of love."

LETHE.

I.

THERE is a scent of roses and spilt wine
   Between the moonlight and the laurel
     coppice ;
The marble idol glimmers on its shrine,
  White as a star, among a heaven of poppies.
Here all my life lies like a spilth of wine.
There is a mouth of music like a lute,
  A nightingale that singeth to one flower ;
Between the falling flower and the fruit,
  Where love hath died, the music of an hour.

2.

To sit alone with memory and a rose ;
  To dwell with shadows of whilom romances ;
To make one hour of a year of woes,
  And walk on starlight, in ethereal trances,

With one fair face white as a moon-white rose :
To win from music's body and the bud's
    A spirit and an essence of sweet fire,
Between the heart-beat's burning and the blood's,
    Is part of love and of the dream's desire.

3.

There is a song to silence and the stars
    From virgin lips a first love's passion parches ;
And down the stream of night, like nenuphars,
    The tossing fires of their cedar torches.
Here all my life dreams lonely as the stars.
Shall not one hour of all those hours suffice
    For resignation, God hath given as dower ?
Between the summons and the sacrifice
    One hour of love, th' eternity of an hour ?

4.

The shrine is shattered and the bird is gone ;
    Dark is the house of music and of bridal ;
The stars are stricken and the storm sweeps on ;
    White, 'neath a wreck of roses, lies the idol,

Sad as the memory of a joy that 's gone :
To dwell with slumber while the fingers kiss
    To dreams one last chord of love's broken lyre,
Between remembering and forgetting, this
    Is part of life and of the world's desire.

LOTUS.

WHERE is the vale and mountain,
    And where the rock and stream,
    That held one life of music,
  Another life of gleam ;
Where she and I were shadows
  And all our world, a dream ?

A thousand spells for waking,
  And only two for sleep :
The first of these is sorrow
  Of love that can not weep :
The other one is terror
  Of love no man would keep.

And was it in the valley,
  Where all the sad wind saith,
Is " I am weary, weary,"
  That I heard her whisper, " Death " ?

As if upon pale eyelids
  The Beautiful breathed its breath.

There was no tomb before us,
  Nor any stone to tell
Of love, or hate, or horror
  In heaven or in hell—
But on her lips the legend,
  And in her eyes the spell.

And was it on the mountain,
  The stealthy stars have crossed
To stand austere with silence,
  That I heard her murmur, " Lost " ?
As if dark eyes one moment
  The Terrible should accost.

There was no memoried presence
  Of flower or star or bird
To tell of tears and parting
  That heartbreak once had heard—
But in her face the vision,
  And in her heart the word.

Where is the vale and mountain,
  And where the rock and stream,
That held one life of music,
  Another life of gleam,
Where she and I were shadows
  And all our world, a dream?

MOLY.

WHEN by the wall the tiger-flower swings
    A head of sultry slumber and aroma ;
    And by the path, whereon the blown
       rose flings
Its obsolete beauty, the long lilies foam a
White place of perfume, like a beautiful breast ;
Between the pansy fire of the west,
And poppy mist of moonrise in the east,
      This heartache will have ceased.

The witchcraft of soft music and sweet sleep—
    Let it beguile the burthen from my spirit,
And white dreams reap me, as strong reapers reap
    The golden grain and gorgeous blossom near it ;
Let me behold how gladness gives the whole
The transformed countenance of my own soul ;
Between the sunset and the risen moon,
      Let sorrow vanish soon.

And these things then shall keep me company :
   The eye-glance of the dew ; the look and laughter
Of flower and bird ; the soul and sorcery
   Of every wind and water reaching after
The secret of the stars, to glass a guess ;
These of themselves shall shape my happiness,
A visible presence I shall lean upon,
      Feeling that care is gone.

Forgetting how the cankered flower must die ;
   The unripe fruit fall, sicklied to its syrup ;
How joy, begotten 'twixt a sigh and sigh,
   Waits with one foot forever in the stirrup ;—
Remembering how within the hollow lute
Soft music sleeps when music's voice is mute ;
And in the heart, when all seems wild despair,
      Hope still sits waiting there.

POPPY AND MANDRAGORA.

LIFE shall not keep me here :
    Here there is sadness in the early
      year ;
Here sorrow comes where joy went laughing late ;
The sicklied face of heaven hangs like hate
Above the woodland and the meadow land ;
And Spring hath taken fire in her hand
Of frost and made a dead bloom of her face,
Which was a flower of chastity and grace,
And light's serenest fragrance long ago.
    Life shall not keep me, no !

    I shall go far away
Into the sunrise of a calmer day :
Where all the nights resign them to the moon,
And drug their hearts with odor and soft tune,
And speak dim dreams in starlight ; where the
    hours

Teach immortality with fadeless flowers ;
And all the day the bee delights the bloom,
And all the night the moth spills strange perfume
From bell and bugle, like an influence.
        I shall go far from hence.

        Why should I sit and weep,
And yearn with heavy eyelids still to sleep ?
Forever hiding from my heart the fate,
Death within death, life doth accumulate,
Like winter snows, along the barren leas
And sterile hills, whereon no lover sees
The crocus limn the beautiful in flame ;
The hyacinth and jonquil write the name
Of God in fire, with a certain eye.
        Why should I sit and sigh ?

        I will not stay and long,
Here where my soul is wasting for a song ;
Where no bird sings ; and far beneath the stars
No silver water strikes melodious bars ;
And in the rocks and forest-haggard hills
No quick-tongued echo from her grotto fills

With eery syllables the solitude—
The vocal image of the voice which wooed—
She, of sweet sound the elfin looking-glass,
    Sick with life's sad Alas!

    What should I say to her?
A hollow-eyed, a sad-faced wanderer,
Love looks not on, nor gives one thought unto :—
Love, busy with the birth of bud and dew,
And vague gold wings within the chrysalis ;
Who will not miss me, nor the timid kiss
She knew not of, who had no kiss for me
Who gave my heart to her in poesy,
A gift of love, a boon of burgeoning.
    What should I say or sing?

    I shall go far away.
She will not care, who murders thus my day
With the dark daggers of neglectful eyes,
Lips' sword of silence ! . . .   Had she sighed me
    lies,
Not passionate, yet falsely tremulous ;
And lent her mouth to mine, in mockery ; thus

Smiled from calm eyes a scornful negative ;
Then, then my heart had taught itself to live,
Feeding its love on her indifference.
     But no !—and I will hence.

     So be the Bible shut
Of all her beauty, and her wisdom but
A clasp of memory !   I shall not seek
The light that came not when the soul was weak
With waiting, and the darkness gave no sign
Of star-born comfort.   Nay ! why should I pine
For psalms of patience and hosannas of
Sad hope and dreary canticles of love ?—
Leave me alone.   My soul hath long supposed
     For me God's book was closed.

NIGHTSHADE.

I.

SINCE she hath lifted up my face to hers,
　　And kissed the lips of worship she denied,
　　　　There is no mouth of verse,
Here in the shadow of the crucified,
Or voice of love, to tell her mine hath died,
　　　　To tell her and to curse !—
She asks me now for flowers that are ashes,
　　Here where the red flow'r of my life lies slain ;
For love, that lashed me once and now that lashes
　　　　Itself in vain.

II.

Since she hath gazed into mine eyes and said,
" Belovèd, look thou in my soul and see,"
　　　　And I have looked and read
The burthen of a kindred Calvary,

I am grown glad that this hath come to be
    Between the quick and dead.—
She asks me now for songs, that only falter,
  Here where the music of my life is hushed ;
For love, that died upon the iron altar
    Where hers lies crushed.

III.

Since she hath touched hot lips to mine and wept,
From out the hell of her own soul, fierce tears,
    Each little look love kept
Of her disdain, unknowingly these years,
And word of scorn, is crier at mine ears
    To wake the hate that slept.—
She asks me now for water that shall cherish,
  When hot sands choke my life's dry fountain-
    head ;
For love, that stirs not though her love should
  perish
    Where mine lies dead.

ROSEMARY.

I.

SHE shall but breathe her wild breath in my
    face,
    She shall but shake her wild hair past mine
      eyes,
    When life sits tearless in grief's sunless cham-
      ber ;
And through the fire of revealing space,
    The marvel of her love shall bid me rise
      And claim her.

II.

This shall not be until within my soul
    Joy's voice is dumb, and broke the instrument,
      And love lies dead beside one withered flower ;
And dark the windows of the home of dole—
    Whence the last flicker of life's taper went—
      Shall tower.

III.

She shall but bend her open eyes on mine,
  She shall but lend one open thought to me,
    When life sits sleepless in sleep's caverned
      hollow ;
And in the night a sudden star shall shine,
  And love shall rise in whiter mystery
    And follow.

IV.

This shall not be until within my heart
  Hope's lips are still, and song that suffereth,
    And love lies dead beside his silent numbers ;
And in the halls of silence, all apart,
  Oblivion sits with the dead face of death
    And slumbers.

AT TWILIGHT.

ONCE more she holds me with her pensive
 eyes,
 Once more I feel her voice's witchery
Within my heart unfountain tears and sighs,
  And fill the soul of me.

Once more she bends a silent face above ;
 Once more I feel her hands' soft touches shake
My life, unbinding long-imprisoned love,
  Bidding my lost dreams wake.

Once more I see her serious smile ; and touch
 Once more the lips of her whose kisses say—
" The night was long, and thou hast suffered much :
  At last, dear heart, 't is day ! "

DAY AND NIGHT.

THEY say to me, the days are not so far off
    When she will come and stay a day with me,
  A day of dreams, till twilight's lonely star, off
The old-time hills, dips dewy to the sea.

Ah, no ! not this !—One night, that gave its soul of
    Calm beauty to the earth ! as she did give
Her love's white starlight to the rugged whole of
  My haggard world and bade me see and live.

I want no days ! when all my soul recalls but
    The revelations of the midnight sky !
No days ! whose hours are as narrow walls,—but
  Of whiter shadow,—where we toil and die.

The day is error's : it can but deceive us
    With shows of Earth, blind with the primal curse.
The night is truth's : its myriad fires weave us
  The thoughts of God, the visible universe.

REVELATION.

I WRITE these things that men may hear.

This was the word that gave me cheer :
There sate a dæmon at mine ear,
Who whispered me, "Man knoweth naught—
First know thyself wouldst thou know aught."

This was the word that brought me grace :
There fell a shape before my face,
Who motioned me, "All forms are sin's—
He aims above himself who wins."

This was the word that made me wise :
There stood an angel at mine eyes,
Who looked, "The world lives selfishly—
Give thy own self if thou wouldst see."

These are the words they brought to me.

SYMBOLIC.

THE trees before the coming storm
    Leap, mad as shrieking Corybants
Who toss to Cybele an arm
    Of rapture, and a face that pants
    Through hair the ritual frenzy slants.

Vague, stormy shapes of tempest sit,
    August, majestic and immense,
Beneath the stars ; as, levin-lit,
    A god might give wild audience
    To awe and night and violence.

Storm is her signet ; hers, who writes
    Stern laws in lightning ; shadowy,
With thunder seals the rolled-out nights,
    And sits in terrible mystery,
    The mountain-crownèd Cybele.

ARGONAUTS.

WITH argosies of dawn he sails,
   And triremes of the dusk,
The Seas of Song, whereon the gales
   Are summers breathing musk.

He hears the hail of Siren bands
   On headlands sunset-kissed ;
The Lotus-eaters wave pale hands
   Within a land of mist.

For many a league he hears the roar
   Of the Symplegades ;
And through the far foam of its shore
   The Isle of Circe sees.

All day he looks with hazy lids
   As sea-gods cleave the deep ;
All night he hears the Nereids
   Sing their wild eyes to sleep.

When heaven thunders overhead,
   And hell upheaves the vast,
Dim faces of the ocean's dead
   Mock him from every mast.

He but repeats the oracle
   That bade him first set sail ;
And cheers his soul with, " It is well !
   Go on ! I shall not fail ! "

Behold ! he sails no earthly barque,
   And on no earthly sea ;
Adown the years he sails the dark
   Deeps of futurity.

Ideals are the ships of Greece
   His purpose steers afar ;
The skies, his seas ; the Golden Fleece
   He seeks, the farthest star.

THE KNIGHT-ERRANT.

THE witch-elm shivers in the gale,
  The thorn-tree's top is bowed ;
The night is black with rain and hail,
  And mist and cloud.

The winds, upon the woods and fields,
  Are swords two fiends unsheathe,
Two fiends, that snarl behind their shields
  And grind their teeth.

The fox-fire, in a haunted place,
  As I ride on and on,
Gleams like a sudden dead-man's face
  And then is gone.

The owl shrieks from the splintered pine
  Demonic ridicule ;
I hear the wild wolf howl and whine
  And splash the pool.

Black bats beat blindly by my eyes
  Like death's own horrible hands ;
The quest leads under hideous skies
    To hideous lands.

I ride with fire upon my casque,
  And fire upon my spear,
The roadway of my soul-set task,
    And know no fear.

Song steels the sinews of my steed,
  And tempers my straight sword ;
I ride the causeway of my creed
    Without a word.

No man shall make the iron pause
  In gauntlet and in thew ;
I ride the highway of God's cause
    To die or do.

My purpose leads me, like a flame,
  'Mid wisps that haunt the fen,
To castle walls of wrong and shame
    And blood-fed men.

Faith's are the lips that wind the horn
    Before the gates of lust ;
Though fifty dragons hiss it scorn,
      Still shall it trust.

Truth's is the hand that thunders at
    The entrances of night ;
Though ten score devils dash it flat,
      Still shall it fight.

Love's are the eyes whose might shall thrill
    The portals vast of sin ;
A thousand deaths may rise to kill,
      Still shall it win.

IN SHADOW.

I.

A MOTH sucks in a flaming flower :
    The moon beams on the old church-tower :
I watch the moth and waning moon—
    A moth-white slip—
    One silver tip
In ghostly tree-tops, drifting soon
To gleam above the church an hour.

II.

The gray moth on the dewy pod
Dreams ; and the sleepy poppies nod
    Their drugged heads in the balmy breeze,
        That loves to sing
        Of wave and wing,
    And, drowsing in the purple trees,
Drops snowy petals on the sod.

III.

My soul dreams at life's blood-red heart
Of that thou art ; of thee, who art
  All silence ; saying something rare
      As spirits know
      When lilies blow
  Beneath sweet heaven ;—phantom-fair,
The beauty thou hast grown a part.

IV.

My soul is sad as any bloom
The moonlight haunts beside a tomb ;
  So very weary with the love
      No words may speak—
      Oh, wild and weak !—
  Here where thy tombstone's marble dove
Makes of the moonlight plaintive gloom.

LEGENDARY.

I.

IT was a gipsy maiden
　　Within the forest green ;
　　It was a gipsy maiden
　　Who shook a tambourine :
The star of eve had not the face,
The woodland wind had not the grace
　　　　Of Flamencine.

II.

Her bodice was of purple,
　　Her shoes of satin sheen ;
Her bodice was of purple
　　With scarlet laid between :
The dew of dusk was in the tread,
The black of night was on the head
　　　　Of Flamencine.

III.

Among the dreaming vistas,
    The darkling dells between,
Among the dreaming vistas
    I heard her tambourine :
And far within the ghostly glade
The moonbeams and the shadows play'd
        Round Flamencine.

IV.

Among the beechen shadows
    When fire-flies are seen,
Among the beechen shadows
    When glow-worms glimmer green,
Then down the darkness like a light
She dances ; and the eyes are bright
        Of Flamencine.

V.

There is a gipsy maiden
    Within the forest green ;

There is a gipsy maiden
 Who shakes a tambourine :
These many years I am her slave ;—
The violets grow upon the grave
 Of Flamencine.

THE MILL WATER.

THE water-flag and wild cane grows
　　Round banks whereon the sunlight sows
Fantastic gold when, on its shores,
The wind sighs through the sycamores.

In one green angle, just in reach,
Between a willow-tree and beech,
Moss-grown and leaky lies a boat
The thick-grown lilies keep afloat.

And where the wild-grapes build a brake
Still swims the spotted water-snake ;
And from the hills, a gray blue streak
Soars down the gaunt fly-up-the-creek.

Between the lily-pads and blooms
The water-spirits set their looms,
To weave the restless lace that dims
The glimmering leaves of under limbs.

Each lily is the hiding place
Of some gray witch-thing's elfish face,
That watches you with gold-green eyes
Where bubbles of its breathing rise.

I fancy, when the waxing moon
Leans through the trees and dreams of June ;
And when the black bat slants its wing,
And lonelier the green-frogs sing ;

I fancy, when the whippoorwill
In some old tree sings wild and shrill,
With glow-worm eyes that dot the dark,—
Each holding high a firefly spark

To torch its way,—the witch-things come :
And some float rocking here ; and some
Unmoor the lily leaves and oar
Around the old boat on the shore.

They climb through oozy weeds and moss ;
They swarm its rotting sides and toss
Their firefly torches o'er its edge,
Or hang them in the tangled sedge.

The boat is loosed. The moon is pale.
Around the dam they slowly sail.
Upon the bow, to pilot it,
A ghastly will-o'-the-wisp doth sit.

And have I seen it all in dreams ?
Or more ? forgotten !—For, it seems,
Beneath the stern . . . what saw I there ?—
A woman's face with weedy hair !

EIDOLONS.

THE white moth-mullein thrust its slim
   Cool, fairy flowers around his knee ;
In places where the way lay dim
   The tree-tops, arching suddenly,
Made tomb-like mystery for him.

The wild-rose and the elder, drenched
   With rain, perfumed a misty place,—
As if the ghost of sorrow blenched
   Pale raiment fragrant past his face,
Who walked with white lips closed and clenched.

And far within the forest, where
   Weird shadows stood like murdered men,
And where the ground-hog dug its lair,
   The she-fox whelped and had its den,—
Was it his own voice crying there?

One dead trunk, like a ruined tower,
  Dark green with toppling trailers, shoved
Its wild wreck o'er the brush ; one bower
  Looked like a dead knight casqued and gloved
In starlit steel that haunted hour.

Now, near, the strange voice spake him ; thin
  As echoes of a thought that sings
To sleep ; and, sitting with his chin
  Upon his palm—was it the wings
Of owls that shuddered out and in ?

And now the voice was still ; and slow,
  With eyes that stared on naught but night,
He looked and saw—what none shall know !
  His soul's reflection, wild and white ?
Or form of immaterial woe ?

And men who found him,—weary led
  By the wild fox,—within that place
Saw in his staring eyes, 't is said,
  The thing he met there face to face,
The thing that left him sitting dead.

UNDER DARK SKIES.

I.

HILLS rolled in woods, that lair the owl and
    fox ;
Harsh fields, that fall before the woods' advance
As wild-men fly from hunters, tossing locks
    Through which their eyes of yellow fire glance ;
Great blurs of briers and lugubrious rocks,—
    Like crumbled blackness,—with a pool beneath,
    Whereon the wisps, like something evil, dance ;
And then a house, like the wrecked face of death.

II.

There where the moon hangs sinister, o'er parched
    And haggard thorns,—a golden battle-bow,
Or shield of bronze, God's wars have scarred and
      scorched,—
    What crime hath cursed it . . . who shall
      ever know ?

—Night only! Night with eyeless eyes, who
    torched
And felt the stigma of its branded sod,
As from the pool a ghastly face rose slow
Beneath the storm and rushing fire of God.

THE SECRET.

SHE stands within the stormy glow
   Of sunset, with a face of snow,
The white embodiment of woe,
     As night comes on.

She stands within the sombre glare
Of dusk, with dark neglected hair,
An apparition of despair,
     When day is gone.

The hideous house within the vale
Looks spectral as a ragged sail
The Dutchman hoists against the gale
     On haunted seas.

And in the garden,—one vast brake
Of dock and thistle,—snail and snake
Crawl ; and the death-watch lies awake
     Among the trees.

The stagnant stream along the night
Creeps, like a nightmare, where each white
Lily seems an uneasy light
    By goblins tossed.

And through the cypress-trees and vines
The red-fox skulks and laps and whines ;
The owl hoots, and its eyeball shines
    In darkness lost.

She stands beside the sleepy stream ;
Her garment drips at every seam ;
She seems a shadow in a dream
    Of death and woe.

No star stares half so steadily
On earth as in the stream stares she ;
And what she sees there, it may be
    The owls—they know.

PHANTOMS.

THIS was her home ; one mossy gable thrust
　　Above the cedars and the locust trees :
This was her home, whose beauty now is dust,
　A lonely memory for melodies
　The wild birds sing, the wild birds and the bees.

Here every evening is a prayer : no boast
　Or ruin of sunset makes the wan world wroth ;
Where, through the twilight, like a pale flower's
　　　ghost,
　A drowsy flutter, flies the tiger-moth ;
　And dusk spreads darkness like a dewy cloth.

In vagabond velvet, all the placid day,
　A stain of crimson, lolled the butterfly ;
The south-wind sowed with ripple and with ray
　The pleasant waters ; and the gentle sky
　Looked on his gladness like a quiet eye.

Its melancholy quaver, lone and low,
  The gray tree-toad at gloaming will repeat ;
The whippoorwill, far in the afterglow,
  Complain to silence ; and the lightning beat,
  In one still cloud, glimmers of golden heat.

He comes not yet. Not till the dusk be dead,
  And all the western glow be far withdrawn ;
Not till,—a sleepy mouth love's kiss makes red,—
  The baby bud opes in a rosy yawn,
  Breathing sweet guesses at the dreamed-of dawn.

When in the shadows, like a rain of gold,
  The fire-flies stream steadily ; and bright
Along the moss the glow-worm, as of old,
  A crawling sparkle—like a crooked light
  In smoldering vellum—scrawls a square of night :

Then, ghost of his dead love ! dost lean to him,
  Within a space that hath not any place,
Between the starlight and his eyes ; so dim
  With suave control and soul-compelling grace,
  He can not help but see thee, face to face.

THREE BIRDS.

A RED-BIRD sang upon the bough
   When wind-flowers nodded in the dew ;
My spring of bird and flower wast thou,
   O tried and true !

A brown bird warbled on the wing
   When poppy buds were hearts of heat ;
I wooed thee with a golden ring,
   O sad and sweet !

A black-bird twittered in the mist
   When nightshade blooms were filled with frost ;
The leaves upon thy grave are whist,
   O loved and lost !

IDENTITIES.

I SAT alone in the manor room
  Of beautiful Sin in her winding shroud ;
The night was stricken with glare and gloom,
    And the haunted wind was loud.

I heard the gallop of one who rode
  Like the sough of leaves that the rain-wind
      crisps ;
The night with the speed of her steed was sowed
    With streaming will-o'-the-wisps.

And it cried in me, "'T is a long-lost Shame,
  Who rides to thy house through the night and
      rain !
She will blaze in the blackness a face of flame
    When she opens thy door again !"

I thought of the blame of her lips and brow ;
  And stared at the door she must enter in

To sear my soul with her eyes, and bow
　　My heart by the corpse of Sin.

As hushed as the mansion of death was night,
　When, dark as a sob of the storm, she came—
But her face, like beautiful Sin's, was white,
　　And her face and Sin's—the same !

A VISION.

(AS IT WAS GIVEN TO ME IN SLEEP.)

I.

STARLESS and still and lustreless
  And sombre black, it seemed to me,
  The heaven hung in hideousness
  Of Hell's serenity.
Indefinite and vague and old
  As nothing that is ours,
It rose with steeples, dark with mold,
  Like two colossal towers.

II.

Infernal monsters crumbled 'mid
  The trefoils of its dim façade,

And, hideous as murder, hid
  Gnarled in the pillared shade.
And all below and overhead,
  In cancerous blotches, grew
The gray gangrene of lichens dead,
  And fungi, sickly blue.

III.

Beneath the black impending skies,
  Weird as Death's countenance it stood,
Hollow, with vacant window eyes
  Staring on solitude.
The grass was black ; the gravestones white ;
  A weary white were they ;
And league on league along the night
  Like phantoms stretched away.

IV.

And I, who entered in, could hear
  No organ notes resound and roll ;

The presence of an awful fear
  Stood unseen near my soul.
And, lo ! I saw, like Hell's wild songs,
  The vast interior carved
With stony shapes of women throngs,
  Naked, obscene, and starved.

V.

Medusa mouths and Harpy hands,
  Dead eyes, in which the Graeæ nod ;
Like idols, wherein heathen lands
  Image the plague's black god.
Round archèd door and window-frame,
  On floor and vault, behold,
The chiselled forms were all the same !
  Gray with exuding mold.

VI.

And I, who entered in, unled,
  Could hear no sweet voice lift the hymn ;

But felt th' effluvia of the dead
   Around my senses swim—
Miasms, that rotted from their waves
   This horrible eminence,
Where, throned upon a thousand graves,
   Death dreams of pestilence.

THE NORMAN KNIGHT.

WITHIN the castle chamber
    The Norman knight lay dead ;
The quarterings of the casement
    Shone holy round his head.

And first there came a maiden ;
    Her face was wet and white ;
She kissed his mouth and murmured,
    " Thou wast my own true knight."

Within the arrased chamber
    The Norman knight lay dead ;
And tapers four and twenty
    Burnt at his feet and head.

And next there came a friar
    And prayed beside his bier ;
" Thou art a blessèd angel,
    Who wast so noble here."

Within the lofty chamber
  The Norman knight lay dead ;
Dim through the carven casement
  The moonbeams lit his head.

And then there came a varlet—
  Loud laughed he in his face :
"Thus do I spit upon thee,
  Thee and thy cursèd race ! "

Within the silent chamber
  The Norman knight lay dead—
Nor Norman knight nor Saxon serf
  Heard what the dead man said.

THE SALAMANDER.

(LOVE DÆMONIC.)

ONCE she breathed upon my eyes,
    Touched the soul that dreamed within
  me ;
All the magic that might win me
  Whispered to my heart with sighs—
  Darkness can not make them lies ! . . .
    Bring me moly, hellebore !
Mix them for my soul's nepenthe,
For my spirit's dread Amenti,
    For the curse which comes once more
    With unutterable lore !

  Sunlight, starlight or the moon,
Stormlight, firelight or the sheening
Witchlight, realize no meaning
  Of her glory's plenilune ;

Of her self's unriddled rune,
    And most awful beauty ! nor
Actual, nor yet ideal !—
Mortal and immortal real !
    Of the red heat, of the star,
    And no part of what these are !—

I am hers and—woe is mine !
Has she drugged me with the gladness
Of some elemental madness ?—
    Like a demigod I pine
    'Twixt the mortal and divine.—
    When I see her, lo, she stands
In the luminous electre
Of a star : a smiling spectre
    With white scintillating hands
    Luring to unhallowed lands.

And I see, in fearful file,
A mirage of tower and terrace,
Lawn, and mountain range, that buries
    Flame in frost, loom ; mile on mile
    Gleams the crescent of her isle :
9

Where the lurid waters lull
Shores that roll the rainbow fire ;
Sweet with living lute and lyre,
   'Neath the rose-red guiding gull,
   Glides her star-like galley's hull.

Wind-like shapes the slaves who row
Us where rise her walls of amber,
Towers of vivid ruby clamber
   Over terraces below
   Summits of refulgent snow :
    Lambent lazuli and shell
Portals ; courts with sunset marbled,
Where the lightning fountains warbled
   Out of basined pearl and fell
   Into hollowed curbuncle.

Rosy silver is the skin
Of her reaching arm commanding,
With its shapely hand, me, standing
   At her gates, to enter in,
   Burning as a Seraphin.—

Limpid blackness are her eyes,
Where the frozen fire smolders ;
And upon her shining shoulders,
  Like a tangible glitter, lies
  Hair voluptuous topaz dyes.

  Mouth of sibilant soft flame ;
Lilith lips, whose language brightens
With illusive love, that lightens
  Into music and the name
  Of desire no man shall tame :
    Passion and the thoughts that wed
Love and languor; and caresses
Of sweet touch whose kiss expresses
  Love, that dreams have lured and led ;
  Love, upon which dreams are fed.

  She has touched me with her lips ;
Kissed me at her palace portal ;
And the fire, which is immortal,
  All that 's mortal in me sips—
  Ah, the spirit-part's eclipse !

As when moon and planet swoon
Unto each ; the world is kindled
Strangely ; while the disc is dwindled
    Of the earth-o'ershadowed moon,
    Darkening from lune to lune.

And she laughs ; and leads me where
Cloudy, wild, chameleon color
Marbles halls with hues, the duller
    For her astral presence there,
    Beaming white with beaming hair :
    Where in roses purple pale,—
Dropping like a ruby bubble
Through the moon dust,—" Double, double,"
    Throbs the crimson nightingale ;
    And its song—a fiery trail.

Gardens where the scarlet snake
Coils beneath the flaming flowers ;
Where the musk mimosa bowers
    Vague vermilion shadows make
    In the coruscating lake :

Where the brilliant moths go by
Like great diamonds ; opal-burning
Butterflies ; and rainbow-turning
　　Peacock-spangled newts, that vie
　　With the rocks whereon they lie.

Constellated moss which fills
Banks with lustre ; where the leaden
Lichen and the fungus redden,
　　And the sparkling orchid spills
　　Gleaming globules on the hills :
　　Where, in iridescent light,
Glow the golden-checkered zinnias ;
Blazing bugles, the gloxinias
　　Burn a radiant red and white,
　　Making morning of each height.

I have gazed in eyes not mine,
Where the liquid moonlight glittered
Of the rivers that were littered
　　With the grail, like prisms in wine,
　　Angles of seductive shine :

Where, in sunset-colored moss,
Glow-worms, smoldering emeralds, twinkled ;
And the blood-red shade was sprinkled
   With convulsive sapphire gloss
   Where the fire-flies rained across.

Where the reeds made rays of rose,
And white mirrored moons, the lotus—
Like a spirit giving notice
   Of the unseen light which glows
   Where the under water flows—
     Dreams have met us on the way ;
Where, like an auroral splendor,
Rolled the forest, soft and tender
   As the light of dying day,
   Moon-crowned dreams, who bade us stay.

Through the violetish light,
Winged with nautilus and lily
Fire, adown the forest's stilly
   Vistas, starry whirls of white,
   Floated birds with eyes of night.

I must follow where she leads—
Blinding portals of her castle
To my entering feet are facile . . .
    Love no terrible trumpet needs
    At such gates to bugle deeds.

    Lo, my reason never veils
Thoughts from her.   To her caresses
All my heart knows it confesses
    With a faith that never fails,
    Though it hears the truth which wails
        In its soul's admonishment,
Of the curse which sits in session
In each amorous confession
        Of her beauty's indolent
        Love, which nothing angel sent.

    I have drained the feverish cup
Of all darkness !   Made a leman
Of an elemental demon,
    While my soul stood staring up
    Drinking poison at each sup !—

While she smiles on me, 't is well.
I shall follow, though she take me
Out of conscience ; ne'er to wake me
    From the dream of asphodel
    To the curse—yea ! it is well !

And her wine's mesmeric gold
Of clairvoyance,—that romances
In informing Protean fancies
    With a beauty never old,
    And emotion never cold,—
      She will bring me if I wake
From the trances which environ
Me, and 'neath the subtle siren
    See the demon's dreaming snake
    With destroying eyes that ache :—

While the slow laconic look
    Of her eyes bespeak no censure ;
    Languid eyes, which still adventure
Ways her serpent fancy took,
Wiser than the wisest book :

And my soul shall reverence
Her,—whose gaze is God's negation,—
Seeing, like an emanation,
   All she dreams—an influence
   Of mirage that chains each sense.

And her eyes shall seem to say :
" One more dream before the morning !
Since thy soul hath given warning,
   One more dream ere break of day !
   One more dream and then away ! "
   And my soul shall never see,
Till her basilisk beauty flashes,
And the curse from out the ashes
   Of her passion suddenly
   Coils around the heart of me.

THE ROSICRUCIAN.

I.

THE tripod flared with a purple spark,
    And the mist hung emerald in the dark :
    Now he stooped to the lilac flame
  Over the glare of the amber embers,
Thrice to utter no earthly name ;
  Thrice, like a mind that half remembers ;
Bathing his face in the magic mist
Where the brilliance burned like an amethyst.

II.

" Sylph, whose soul was born of mine,
Born of the love that made me thine,
Once more flash on the flesh !   Again
  Be the loved caresses taken !
Lip to lip let our mouths remain !—
  Here in the circle of sense, awaken !

Ere spirit meets spirit, the flesh laid by,
Let me know thee, and let me die ! "

III.

Sunset heavens may burn, but never
Bring such splendor !   There bloomed an ever
Opaline orb, where the sylphid rose,
  A shape of luminous white ; diviner
White than the essence of light that sows
  The moons and suns through space ; and finer
Than radiance born of a shooting star,
Or the wild Aurora that streams afar.

IV.

" Look on the face of the soul to whom
Thou givest thy soul like added perfume !.
Thou, who heard'st me who long had prayed,
  Waiting alone at evening's portal !—
Thus on thy lips let my lips be laid,
  Love, who hast made me twice immortal !
Give me thine arms now !   Come and rest
Happiness out on my beaming breast ! "

v.

Was it her soul? or the sapphire fire
That sang like the note of a Seraph's lyre?
Out of her mouth there came no word—
　　She spake with her soul, as a flower speaketh
Fragrant messages none hath heard,
　　Which the sense divines when the spirit seek-
　　　　eth. . . .
And he seemed alone in a place so dim
That the angel's face, who was gazing at him,
For its burning eyes, he could not see—
And he knew he was dead ; and that he and she
Were one—and he saw that this was he.

ARABAH.

A ND one brought pearls and one brought
    passion-flowers
  To blind Arabah as he lay in dreams,
And one brought visions of the after hours :
  So he beheld the rainbow-rolling streams
Of Eden on harmonious sands of gold,
  And battlements builded of prismatic beams.
Nor sightless was he now, nor weak, nor old,
  For, lo ! the dark-eyed girls of Paradise
Leaned kissing him with kisses manifold.—
  Feeble Arabah with unseeing eyes
No longer sightless, since each kiss they gave
  Was youth immortal, love that never dies.—

"Who 's he who lies upon the mosque's cold
    pave ? "—
  "A blind man, whom an angel's hand shall
    lead."—

" A beggar, richer than the rich who have."
" Behold the lesson, such as Sufis feed
The soul upon !—O faith, blind-praying ! see
    Out of thyself how God repays indeed
Ten-thousand fold one generosity ! "

Who knew it not ? how, at the hour of prayer,
A slave beneath each shoulder, it was he,
    Old, blind Arabah, whom a suppliant there,
Footsore and hungry, met and asked for bread.
    " Alas ! my son, God's poor are everywhere,"—
Hoar as a Koreish priest, Arabah said ;—
    " The rich one I though penniless indeed !
Take thou these slaves and sell, and buy thee
        bread."—
    And thrust them from him saying, " Thou hast
        need.
Refuse, and I renounce them ! "—And the wall
    Struck with his staff, saying, " Can this not
        lead ? "—
While from some mosque rang the muezzin's call,
" God is most mighty !   Allah seeth all ! "

NORTH BEACH, FLORIDA.

SURGE upon surge, the miles of surf uncurl
    Volutes of murmur ; and the far shore
        foams ;
The thundering billows, boiling into pearl,
    The wild wind clouds and combs.

Wave upon wave,—as when the Nereids pour
  Green tresses from white fillets, when the arms
Of Tritons reach them racing to the shore,—
    Bursts on the beach that storms.

Oh thou primeval solitude ! that rolled
  Out of creation when the world was young !
And shall roll on when man is not, and old
    The ages yet unsung !

Time shall not flaw thy music !—thou hast heard
  God's spirit on thy waters, and no night

Annuls the memory of that one Word
      Which blossomed into light.

With such impression as upon thy face
    The soaring seagulls make, man comes and
        came ;
And countless myriads, race on warring race,
      Have found thee thus the same.

Thy part is to destroy and still remain
    Immutable 'midst mutability :
The symbol of all change, that clothes again
      Mystery in mystery !

THE WATCHER.

AH, young the dream which held her when
    The world was moon-white with the May ;
She watched the singing fishermen
    Sail out to sea at break of day :
Soft, as the morning heaven then,
    The eyes that watched him sail away.

Ah, calm her grief when summer filled
    The world with warm maturity :
Far off she watched the nets that spilled
    Their twinkling foison by the sea :
And sat upon the cliffs and stilled
    With song the baby on her knee.

Who to her love would make them lies—
    Those vows his sea-slain manhood swore ?
Beneath the raining autumn skies
    The fishing vessels put to shore :
She watches with remembering eyes
    For the brown face that comes no more.
    10

ANALOGIES.

OF Rosamond the beautiful, of her
  The joy and pride of Cunimund,—last
  king
Of the fierce Gepidæ,—a warrior
  Such as the old-world minstrels loved to sing,
To Alboin, Prince of Lombardy,—at war
  With Cunimund her father,—fame did bring
Report of such proud loveliness and grace
That he had loved her ere he saw her face.

War was between them and the hate of thrones :
  For he had slain a son of Turismund
And brother of King Cunimund. His bones
  Were as a wall between desire—unsunned
Of such encouragement as young Love owns ;
  Young Love, before the ruined lips that stunned
Appeal with dead defiance, and the grim
Confrontment mocking as the hopes of him.

Such oft is Life ! that, standing with Despair
  Looks on some crime,—as looked the conqueror
Of Rosamond,—ere goaded on to dare
  Fate by the stern arbitrament of war :
Death smiles within the danger of her hair ;
  Defeat, more deadly than the wild Avar,
Gleams armored in her eyes ; and in her mouth
An exarch marshals legions from the south.

Yet, should he so prevail against her might—
  Her woman Pride, her hosts of beautiful
Angers and Scorns—that she be forced, some
      night,
  To pledge him faith in Hate's full cup, a skull—
What though he sees Revenge writ fiery white
  Upon her brow ! Revenge, that hides a dull
Poison for sleep, or dagger all prepared !—
Life writes not *Failure* where Fate writes
    He dared.

IMITATED FROM OSSIAN.

I.

OINA-MORUL'S LAMENT.

AND singing she said with emotion :
    "Who looks from the surf-sounding rocks
On the white-closing mists of the ocean,
    Like the wing of the raven his locks ?
Dark care on his brow is a furrow ;
    And dark is the grief of his eye ;
But darker than sorrow my sorrow—
    Tonthermod, my love, must thou die !—
From Malorchul's high hall I will wander
    To islands unknown of a barque !
With the race of the sea-kings around her,
    The soul of Oina is dark. . . .
Is the sound of the storm on the ocean,
    Where the darkness is riven with flame ?
Or the voice of Cruth-Loda's emotion

As he boasts in the might of his name ?—
The dark-bosomed ships, bending over,
   Kiss the white-bosomed breasts of the sea—
But thou ! thou art lost, O my lover,
   Tonthermod, forever to me ! "

———

II.

TOSCAR AND COLMADONA.

L IKE the rippling stream of Crona
    Where the forests darken down,
Were the locks of Colmadona
   O'er her white neck falling brown.

And the night lay soft and sable
   Over Carul's druid walls ;
Round the mighty oaken table
   Rang the harps through ancient halls.

With the harp now Carul's daughter
   Blends the music of her voice ;

Like the sound of falling water
In the moonlight is her voice.

Toscar, gazing, leans and listens
To the singing of the maid—
Like a beam that falls and glistens
Where the stormy deep is laid ;

Like a gleam that leaps and lightens
From the midnight clouds that roll,
And the troubled water brightens,—
Came she to his troubled soul. . . .

In the morn they rose and hunted
Through the hills with spear and bow ;
Bleeding by the stream it wonted
Fell the arrow-stricken roe.

Through wild Crona's vale returning,
From the wood a youth drew near ;
On his arm a shield was burning,
In his hand a pointless spear.

"Whence," said Toscar then of Lutha,
  "Comes this flying beam of war?—
Is there peace at wide Colamon
  Round the lovely maid of Car?"

Said the youth, "At wide Colamon
  Colmadona once did dwell,
Fair as any foaming fountain
  Springing in a lonely dell.

"There she dwelt!—Ah, canst thou hear
    it?—
With the King of Lochlin's son,
Luth, who won with love her spirit,
  To the mountains she is gone."

"Stranger," then said Toscar sadly,
  "Hast thou marked the chieftain's path?
He must die!—I loved her madly!—
  He must fall before my wrath!

"Thou art armed . . . Give me thy
    bossy
Shield!" and on it hands he laid—

Lo ! behind it, white and glossy,
   Rose the bosom of a maid.

The high-bosomed Colmadona,
   Carul's blue-eyed daughter there,
Standing by the reedy Crona,
   In her armor very fair.

Warrior-like her love for Toscar
   Led her from her father's hall—
Love will laugh at kings and armies
   In the halls of great Fingal.

1886.

THE BATTLE.

THE night had passed. The day had come,
 Bright-born, into a cloudless sky :
We heard the rolling of the drum,
 And saw the war-flags fly.

And noon had crowded upon morn
 Ere Conflict shook her red locks far,
And blew her brazen battle-horn
 Upon the hills of War.

Noon darkened into dusk—one blot
 Of nightmare lit with hell-born suns ;—
We heard the scream of shell and shot
 And booming of the guns.

On batteries of belching grape
 We saw the thundering cavalry
Spur headlong—iron shape on shape
 Led starlike on to die.

And dusk had moaned itself to night,
  Rain-haunted.   And we slept again—
To dream of many a bivouac light,
  And dark fields vast with slain.

THE MESSAGE.

A DAY of drought foreboding rain and wind,
As if stern heaven, feeling earth had sinned,
   Looked on with hatred. When the evening
      came,
Down in the west,—no sunset fire had thinned,—
   Black as the smoke of battle, flame on flame,

The lightning signalled and the heaven spoke
In thunder, and storm's pent-up torrents broke :—
   She saw the wild night when the dark pane
      flashed ;
Heard, where she stood, the disemboweled oak
   Roar into fragments when the welkin crashed.

Long had she waited for a word.   And, lo,
Anticipation still would not say no :
   He has not written ; he will come to her ;
At dawn !—to-night ! Her heart hath told her so ;
   And so expectancy and love aver.

Hope bids her hear *his* fingers on the pane—
The glass is blurred, she can not see for rain :
   Bids hear *his* horse—the wind is never still :
Bids see *his* cloak, ah ! surely that is plain—
   A torn vine tossing at the window-sill.

Her soul goes forth to meet him : Pale and wet,
She sees his face ; the war-soiled epaulet ;
   The sabre-scar there on the soldier's cheek ;
And now he smiles, and now their lips have met ;
   And now . . . Dear heart ! he fell at Cedar
      Creek.

MOSBY AT HAMILTON.

D OWN Loudon lanes, with swinging reins
　　And clash of spur and sabre,
And bugling of the battle horn,
Six score and eight we rode that morn,
Six score and eight of Southern born,
　　All tried in love and labor.

Full in the sun, at Hamilton,
　　We met the South's invaders ;
Who, over fifteen hundred strong,
'Mid blazing homes had marched along
All night, with Northern shout and song,
　　To crush the rebel raiders.

Down Loudon lanes, with streaming manes,
　　We spurred in wild March weather ;
And all along our war-scarred way
The graves of Southern heroes lay—

11

Our guide-posts to revenge that day,
  As we rode grim together.

Old tales still tell some miracle
  Of saints in holy writing—
But who shall say why hundreds fled
Before the few that Mosby led,
Unless the noblest of our dead
  Charged with us then when fighting !

While Yankee cheers still stunned our ears,
  Of troops at Harper's Ferry ;
While Sheridan led on his Huns,
And Richmond rocked to roaring guns,
We felt the South still had some sons
  She would not scorn to bury.

IN HOSPITAL.

WOUNDED to death he lay and dreamed
  The drums of battle beat afar,
And round the roaring trenches screamed
  The hell of war.

Then woke ; and, weeping, heard no word
  To say a sweetheart bent above ;
Yet, in the white-washed ward was heard
  A song of love.

Lay this upon him in his grave,
  The portrait that he kissed, then sighed
" My mother ! " and " Be brave ! be brave ! "
  Then smiled and died.

IN SILHOUETTE.

I.

THE storm-red sun, through wrecks of wind and
        rain,
   And dead leaves driven from the frantic boughs,
   Where, on the hill-top, stood a gaunt, gray house,
Flashed wildest ruby on each rainy pane.

Then woods grew sadder than remembered grief ;
   And crimson   through   the   woodland's   ruin
        streamed
   The sunset's glare—a furious eye, which seemed
Watching the moon rise like a yellow leaf :

An autumn leaf, blown tattered from the lair
   Of dusk behind the storm-swept hill, whereon
   A lonely woman waited ; darkly drawn
With sombre dress and wind-dishevelled hair.

II.

She—who stands looking with no quiet tears
   For the young face of one she knows is lost,
   While, in her heart, the melancholy frost
Gathers of all the unforgotten years ;—

If she should hear to-night a hurrying horse
   Bring home a more immedicable grief,—
   Wild as the whirling of the withered leaf,—
Than the soiled features of a blood-stained corse?

A shattered shape, who names her his own wife ;
   A soldier—no ! a wreck, that bends at last
   A face, that late made lovely all her past,
And groans, "Live with me ! I am death in life !"

ASSUMPTION.

I.

A MILE of moonlight and the whispering wood;
  A mile of shadow, and the odorous lane ;
One large white star above the quietude
  Like one sweet wish ; and, laughter after pain,
  Wild roses wistful in a web of rain.

II.

No star, no rose, when love assumes the lead !
  No woodsman compass of the skies and rocks,
Tattooed with stars and lichens, shall he need
  To guide him where, among the hollyhocks,
  A blur of moonlight, gleam his sweetheart's locks.

III.

We name it beauty—that permitted part,
  The Love-elected apotheosis
Of Nature, which the god within the heart
  Just touching makes immortal, but by this,—
  A star, a rose,—the memory of a kiss.

CARA MIA.

TO M.

I.

SOFT lips to kiss to sleep,
    Soft eyes to make you dream,
    Soft hands to waken ;
Two sweetest flow'rs to keep,
Soft lips that kiss to sleep ;
Two brightest stars to beam,
Soft eyes that make you dream ;
    Wings that are shaken,
    Soft hands that waken.

II.

Her lips, to give perfume ;
Her eyes, to kindle light ;
    Her hands to hallow ;
To every flow'r in bloom

Her lips shall give perfume ;
In every star at night
Her eyes shall kindle light ;
 Wings that are callow
 Her hands shall hallow.

III.

Who would not love to rest ?
Who would not love to lie ?
 Who would not love them ?
Such flowers on their breast,
Who would not love to rest ?
Such stars within their sky,
Who would not love to lie ?
 Such wings above them,
 Who would not love them ?

ESOTERIC.

I.

WITHIN the old, old forest
    The wind hath whispered me
Thou livest—thou, who warest
  With birds in melody,
And all the wood-way starest
  With flowers fragrantly,
    Thou presence none may see !

II.

If I should seek thee sitting
  Beneath the woodland tree,
The elder blossoms knitting
  In wreaths of witchery,
Between the glimpse and flitting,
  What wouldst thou show to me,
    Thou presence none may see ?

III.

O thou, who, mayhap, hidest
  A flow'r upon the tree ;
Or in a color glidest
  Beyond me secretly ;
Or in a scent abidest,
  A fragrance,—show to me
  The thing my heart would see !

IV.

If I should seek thee dreaming
  Upon the wild-rose lea,
Thy feet and white hands gleaming
  More pollened than the bee,
Between the real and seeming,
  What wouldst thou say to me,
  Thou presence none may see ?

V.

O thou, who, mayhap, talkest
  With birds that sing of thee ;

Or with the water walkest,
  A hidden harmony ;
Or in the sweet wind mockest,
  A music,—say to me
  The thoughts my soul would see !

MNEMONICS.

IT shall not be forgotten
   Of any one who sees,—
The sorrel-flow'r amid the moss,
The wind-flower 'mid the trees.

Though I can but remember
All flowers by *her* face,
That flow'r, which is my life's perfume,
Kin to the wildflow'r race.

It shall not be forgotten
Of any one who looks,—
The falling-star above the hills,
Or imaged in the brooks.

Though I can but remember
The star-fire by *her* eyes,
Those stars, which are my destiny,
Bright sisters to the skies'.

And, oh, the song that follows
The wing-step of the bird !—
It shall not be forgotten
When once such song is heard.

Though I can but remember
All music by *her* words,
That song, which is my heart's response,
Kin to the building bird's.

How shall they be forgotten,
The fair and fugitive,
When in all birds and stars and flowers
Love's intimations live !

THE NAIAD.

SHE sits among the iris stalks
　　Of bubbling brooks ; and leans for hours
　　Among the river's lily flowers,
Or on their whiteness walks :
　Above dark forest pools, lone rocks
　Wall in, she leans with dripping locks,
And listening to the echo, talks
　With her fair face—Iothera.

There is no forest of the hills,
　　No valley of the solitude,
　　Nor fern, nor moss, which may elude
Her searching step that stills :
　She dreams among the wild-rose brakes
　Of fountains that the ripple shakes,
And, dreaming of herself, she fills
　The silence with " Iothera."

And every wind, which haunts the ways
　　Of leaf and bough, once having kissed
　　Her virgin nudity, goes whist

With wonder and with praise :
   There blows no breeze which hath not learned
   Her name's sweet melody, and yearned
To kiss her mouth that laughs and says
   " Iothera, Iothera."

No wild thing of the wood, no bird,
   Or brown or blue, or gold or gray,
   Beneath the sun's or moonlight's ray,
That hath not loved and heard :
   They are her pupil's ; she may say
   No new thing, but, within a day,
They have its music, word for word,
   Harmonious as Iothera.

No man who lives and is not wise
   With love for common flowers and trees,
   Bee, bird and beast, and brook and breeze,
And rocks and hills and skies,—
   Search where he will,—shall ever see
   One flutter of her drapery,
One glimpse of limbs, or hair, or eyes
   Of beautiful Iothera.

THE RED-BIRD.

R ED clouds and reddest flowers,
   And now two redder wings
Swim through the rosy hours ;
Red wings among the flowers ;
   And now the red-bird sings.

God gives the red clouds ripples
   Of flame that seem to split
In rubies and in dripples
Of rose where rills and ripples
   The singing flame that lit.

Red clouds of sundered splendor ;
   God whispered one small word,
Rich, sweet, and wild and tender—
And, in the vibrant splendor,
   The word became a bird.

He flies beneath the garnet
  Of clouds that flame and float,—
When summer hears the hornet
Hum round the plum turned garnet,—
  Heaven's music in his throat.

THE STORM.

A DÆMON glares on the hills,
 The frown of his black brow showing,
The hiss of his fierce breath blowing
Like hail through his beard that it fills.
 The forests are taken ;
 The violent oaks
Are twisted and shaken
 As by chariot spokes,
Where mountains awaken
The hoofs of his yokes
Reined sheer with the strength of his arm—
Ride forth, O spirit of storm !—
 What hope for the sparrow,
 Or nest of the bird !
Where fords were once narrow,
 What hope for the herd !
When arrow on arrow
 He empties the third

Of his quiver against their alarm—
   Descend, O spirit of storm !—
You may measure the might that he brings
   By the welkin which echoes his felloes ;
   By the fork of the lightning, that yellows
The darkness, the sword that he swings.
      The cattle are scattered
        And low from the shore ;
      The roses are shattered
        That grew at the door ;
      The swallows look tattered,
        And twitter and soar,
Made glad with the force of his form—
   Rejoice, O spirit of storm !—
      On levels that sunder
        The might of the main,
      He ploughs with the thunder
        And sows with the rain ;
      No sunbeam shall blunder
        Through black till the plain
Is planted with storm as a farm—
   Sweep on, O spirit of storm !—

His path is the abysm, which heaps
 The wild wind behind him, and hovers
 A whirlwind before, that discovers
The hurricane lair where he sleeps.
  On tempests that wrestle
   God's stars shall descend !
  To guard the good vessel
   From rocks that would rend ;—
  Like mercies that nestle,
   God's stars, to defend
The father and his from all harm—
From thee, O spirit of storm !

MARIE.

I.

MARIE draws near :
      I seem to hear
The shy approach of dreamy innocence :
      As if—brown leaves her crown—
      A dryad should step down
From some dim oak-tree where the woods are dense.

II.

      Marie 's with me :
      I seem to see
The brambles blossom where just touched her
      dress :
         For, as the whole spring glows
         In one wild, woodland rose,
In her for me lives all life's loveliness.

LINES TO M.

WHAT better praise for all her ways,
    Than that all hours her ways illume?
Such brightness as the maiden year
Knows, when God's kindness seems as near
    As flowers whose wisdom 's but to bloom.

Hers the deep hair : a face more fair
    Than gardens June sets blossoming ;
The sunshine of her gladness gleams
In bloom-bright lips and cheeks, and dreams
    Upon her throat's soft coloring.

Her voice is sweet as birds that greet
    With song the coming of the light ;
The serious happy gleam that lies
In the dark lustre of her eyes
    Is as the starlight in the night.

Beyond the sea such girls as she
 It was whom Titian loved to paint
With calm Madonna eyes and hair,
Divinely pale and dim and fair,
 Soft as the halo of a saint.

CIRCE.

THE pillared portals of her home once rose
from out the sea ;
Its casements burnt with green sea-fire of ocean
mystery ;
And all its halls of love were full of mermaid melody.

Its battlements of beauty were a pharos from afar,
To lure the wand'ring seamen like a constellated
star ;—
Life may question ; death is silent ; will it answer
where they are ?

It is enough to know that once love led me with a
lute—
To taste the honey of her soul and of her flesh the
fruit ;
Between the soul and flesh she changed my self into
a brute.

It is enough to know that love once sate me at a
feast—

Her word was bread and oil to me, her kiss was
wine at least ;

Between the word and kiss she changed my self into
a beast.

The marble now is vanished where the columned
wonder rose ;

The billow beats complaining there, a heart of many
woes ;

The sea wind sings uncertain things of what the
siren knows.

Ah me ! you know not how it is with him who once
hath been

A portion of such passion and the slave of such a
queen !

What such possession of her love to his whole life
may mean !

The world of languid attitudes that lured him to
despair ;

Abandonments of beauty that his heart would not
    beware—
A red rose suffering death, to live one hour in her
    hair.

Yea, just to be again to her as music to the lute,
As fragrance to the senses, as to lips the blood-red
    fruit,
Between the soul and flesh again, unto her beauty,
    brute !

Her alabaster stairways and her casements filled
    with light,
Her corridors of melody and colonnades of night
Shall haunt his soul forever with the magic of her
    might !

.

THE PAPHIAN VENUS.

WITH anxious eyes and dry, expectant lips,
 Within the sculptured stoa by the sea,
All day she waited while, like ghostly ships,
 Long clouds rolled over Paphos : the wild bee
Sucked in the sultry poppy, half asleep,
Beside the shepherd and his drowsy sheep.

White-robed she waited day by day ; alone
 With the white temple's shrined concupiscence,
The Paphian goddess on her obscene throne,
 Binding all chastity to violence,
All innocence to lust that feels no shame—
Venus Mylitta born of filth and flame.

So must they haunt her marble portico,
 The devotees of passion, grown as pale
As moonlight streaming through the stormy snow ;
 Dark eyes desirous of the stranger sail,—

The gods shall bring across the Cyprian Sea,—
And him elected to their mastery.

A priestess of the temple came, when eve
  Blazed, like a satrap's triumph, in the west ;
And watched her listening to the ocean's heave,
  Dusk's golden glory on her face and breast,
And in her hair the rosy wind's caress,—
Pitying her dedicated tenderness.

When out of darkness night persuades the stars,
  A dream shall bend above her saying, "Soon
A barque shall come with purple sails and spars,
  Sailing from Tarsus 'neath a low white moon ;
And thou shalt see one in a robe of Tyre
Facing toward thee like the god Desire.

"Rise then ! as, clad in starlight, riseth night—
  Thy nakedness clad on with loveliness !
So shalt thou see him, like the god Delight,
  Breast through the foam and climb the cliff to
      press
Hot lips to thine and lead thee in before
Love's awful presence where ye shall adore."

So at her heart the vision entered in,
　　With lips of lust the lips of song had kissed,
And eyes of passion laughing with sweet sin,
　　A starry splendor robed in amethyst,
Seen like that star set in the glittering gloam—
Venus Mylitta born of fire and foam.

So shall she dream until, near middle night,—
　　When on the blackness of the ocean's rim
The moon, like some war-galleon all alight
　　With blazing battle, from the sea shall swim,—
A shadow, with inviolate eyes that pray,
Severe and sad, shall stoop to her and say :

"So hast thou heard the promises of one,—
　　Of her ! with whom the God of gods is wroth,—
For whom was prophesied at Babylon
　　The second death—Chaldæan Mylidoth !
Whose feet take hold on darkness and despair,
Hissing destruction in her heart and hair !

" Wouldst thou behold the vessel she would bring ?—
　　A wreck ! ten hundred years have smeared with
　　　　slime :

A hulk ! where all abominations cling,
    The spawn and vermin of the seas of time :
Wild waves have rotted it, fierce suns have scorched,
Mad winds have tossed and stormy stars have
        torched.

" Can lust give birth to love ! The vile and foul
    Be mother to beauty ? Lo ! can this thing be ?—
A monster like a man shall rise and howl
    Upon the wreck across the crawling sea,
Then plunge ; and swim unto thee ; like an ape,
A beast all belly—Thou canst not escape ! "

Gone was the shadow with the suffering brow ;
    And in the temple's porch she lay and wept,
Alone with night, the ocean, and her vow.
    Then up the east the moon's full splendor swept,
And, dark between it—wreck ? or argosy ?—
A sudden vessel far away at sea.

METAMORPHOSIS.

BEFORE Love's lofty goddess—Life hath
    toiled
  To form from burning dew and dewy fire—
Who kneel and worship with a heart that 's soiled,
Within the secret temple of Desire ;
Their curse is such : that, even while they pray,
They shall not see, nor shall they know thereof,
Their deity is turned a thing of clay,—
Lust, fashioned in the very form of Love.

BEFORE THE TEMPLE.

AND desolate she sate her down
    Upon the marble of the temple's stair.
    You would have thought her, with her
        eyes of brown
White cheeks and hazel hair,
A dryad dreaming there.

A priest of Bacchus passed, nor stopped
To chide her ; deeming her—whose chiton hid
But half her bosom, and whose girdle dropped—
    Some grief-drowned Bassarid,
    The god of wine had chid.

With wreaths of woodland cyclamen
For Dian's shrine, a shepherdess drew near,
All her young thoughts on vestal beauty, when—
    She dare not look for fear—
    Its visible godhead here !

Fierce lights on shields of bossy brass
And helms of gold, next from the hills deploy
Tall youths of Argos.   And she sees *him* pass,
Flushed with heroic joy,
On towards the siege of Troy.

THE DEAD FAUN.

THE joys that touched thee once be mine !
  The sympathies of sky and sea,
  The friendships of each rock and pine,
That made thy lonely life, ah me !
  In Tempe or in Gargaphie !

Such joy as thou didst feel when first,
  On some wild crag, thou stood'st alone,
To watch the mountain tempest burst,
  With streaming thunder, lightning-sown,
  On Latmos or on Pelion !

Thy awe ! when, crowned with vastness, Night
  And Silence ruled the deep's abyss ;
And through dark leaves thou saw'st the white
  Breasts of the starry maids who kiss
  Pale feet of moony Artemis.

Thy dreams ! when breasting matted weeds
    Of Arethusa, thou didst hear
The music of the wind-swept reeds ;
    And down dim forest-ways drew near
    Shy herds of slim Arcadian deer.

Thy wisdom ! that knew naught but love
    And beauty, with which love is fraught ;
The wisdom of the heart—whereof
    All noblest passions spring—that thought,
    As Nature thinks, " All else is naught."

Thy hope ! wherein to-morrow set
    No shadow ;—hope, that, lacking care
And retrospect, could not regret,
    And bloomed in rainbows everywhere
    Of whilom joys again grown fair.

These were thine all : in all life's moods
    Embracing all of happiness :
And when within thy long-loved woods
    Didst lay thee down to die, no less
    Thy happiness stood by to bless.

APOLLO.

I.

ALL the Lydian notes revealing,
　　Son of Leto, oh, come stealing
As the wind Thessalian rivers
Whisper of ! the wind, that shivers
Every ripple into stars,
Blowing bubble-bars on bars.
Bring the harp that haunts the oaks,
Wherein melody invokes
Naiad music of the fount,
Oread music of the mount ;
And such Satyre song as keeps
Revel on Lycæan steeps,
When Night nods, a Mænad shape
Purple with the staining grape.
Wake the chords that dewy grounds
Echo when no mortal hounds

Bell the hunt, whose spear-point shines
Through Arcadia's tangled vines,
When the half-awakened Dawn,
Dreaming on a mountain lawn,
Lets her golden sandals lie
And walks bare-footed through the sky ;
And by Arethusa's bank,
Swift upon the red hart's flank,
Drives Diana's buskined band
Down the cistus-blooming strand.
Then love's minors, swooning o'er
The mountain hush, the ocean roar,
As Selene, stealing, sails
O'er the Lemnos lakes to vales
Where Endymion dreams and feels
Love her stolen kiss reveals.

II.

Thou hast sung of Helicon :
How the sister Muses won
From the nine Piërides
Empire o'er all harmonies.

Thou hast sung of Tempe's maid,
And the sudden laurel's shade.
Thou hast sung of classic loves,
In the temple-columned groves,
Where the marble altar stands
Rose-heaped by the balmy hands
Of Achaian maiden bands ;
Where the bay-crowned priest lifts up
Wine-wet hands that tilt the cup.
Sung, as wild Amphion sung,
Songs,—Parnassian rocks,—that swung
Each in its lyric niche, and massed
Melodious walls like Thebes'.   And last,
Sung, what wrung forth tears in Hell,
Love—no snake-haired Fears could quell.

III.

Ours shall be no island song,
Suited to a maiden throng,
Dancing with their wreaths of roses
To the double-flute's soft closes !—
But a Nation's ! whose large eyes

With life's liberty are wise,
And consenting sympathies
Of all arts and sciences.
She ! who stands above the storms
With truth's thunders in her arms,
And the star-serenity
Of her hope bound burningly
Round her brow ; and at her knee
The spirit of progress who is shod
With ethereal fire of God. . . .
Yea ! thy last shall still be first—
Some grand epopee to burst
With such organ notes as rang
When the stars of morning sang,
And the Sons of Heaven sent
Shoutings through the firmament ;
As our years have justified
And the stars have prophesied.

1886.

THE FEUD.

ROCKS, trees and rocks ; and down a mossy
    stone
The murmuring ooze and trickle of a stream
Of water, where the mountain spring lies lone,—
    A gleaming cairngorm where the shadows
      dream,—
And one wild road winds like a saffron seam.

Here sang the thrush, whose pure, mellifluous note
    Dropped golden sweetness on the fragrant June ;
Here cat- and blue-bird and wood-sparrow wrote
    Their presence on the silence with a tune ;
And here the fox drank 'neath the mountain moon.

Frail ferns and dewy mosses and dark brush,—
    Impenetrable briers, deep and dense,
And wiry bushes,—brush, that seemed to crush

The struggling saplings with its tangle, whence
Sprawled out the ramble of an old rail-fence.

A wasp buzzed by ; and then a butterfly
  In orange and amber, like a floating flame ;
And then a man, hard-eyed and very sly,
  Gaunt-cheeked and haggard and a little lame,
With an old rifle, down the mountain came.

He listened, drinking from a flask he took
  Out of the ragged pocket of his coat ;
Then all around him cast a stealthy look ;
  Lay down ; and watched an eagle soar and float,
His fingers hidden in his hairy throat.

The shades grew longer ; and each Cumberland
    height
  Loomed framed in splendors of the dolphin
    dusk.
Around the road a horseman rode in sight ;
  Young, tall, blond-bearded. Silent, grim and
    brusque,
He in the thicket aimed—Quick, harsh, then husk,

The echoes barked among the hills and made
   Repeated instants of the shot's distress ;—
Then silence—and the trampled bushes swayed ;—
   Then silence, packed with murder—and the press
Of distant hoofs that galloped riderless.

THE RAID.

I.

FAR in the forest, where the rude road winds
  Through twisted briers and weeds, stamped
    down and caked
With mountain mire, the clashing boughs are
    raked
Again with rain whose sobbing frenzy blinds.

There is a noise of winds; a gasp and gulp
  Of swollen torrents; and the sodden smell
  Of woodland soil, dead trees—that long since
    fell
Among the moss—red-rotted into pulp.

Fogged by the rain, far up the mountain glen,
  Deep in the dark, an elfish wisp of light;
  And stealthy shadows stealing through the night
With strong, set faces of determined men.

II.

'Twixt fog and fire, in pomps of chrysoprase,
   Above vague peaks, the morning hesitates
   Ere, o'er the threshold of her golden gates,
Her chariot speeds the splendor of its rays.

A gleaming glimmer in the sun-speared mist,
   A cataract, reverberating, falls :
   Upon a pine a gray hawk sits and calls,
Then soars away, no bigger than the fist.

Along the wild path, through the oaks and firs,—
   Rocks, where the rattler coils itself and suns,—
   Big-booted, belted, and with twinkling guns,
The posse marches with three moonshiners.

DEAD MAN'S RUN.

HE rode adown the autumn wood,
A man dark-eyed and brown ;
A mountain girl before him stood
Clad in a homespun gown.

"To ride this road is death for you !
My father waits you there ;
My father and my brother, too.—
You know the oath they swear."

He holds her by one berry-brown wrist,
And by one berry-brown hand ;
And he hath laughed at her and kissed
Her cheek the sun hath tanned.

"The feud is to the death, sweetheart ;
But forward will I ride."
"And if you ride to death, sweetheart,
My place is at your side."

Low hath he laughed again and kissed
  And helped her with his hand ;
And they have rode into the mist
  That belts the autumn land.

And they had passed by Devil's Den,
  And come to Dead Man's Run,
When in the brush rose up two men,
  Each with a levelled gun.

"Down, down ! my sister !" cries the one ;—
  She gives the reins a twirl ;—
The other shouts, "He shot my son !
  And now he steals my girl !"

The rifles crack : she will not wail :
  He will not cease to ride :
But, oh ! her face is pale, is pale,
  And the red blood stains her side.

"Sit fast, sit fast by me, sweetheart !
  The road is rough to ride !"—
The road is rough by gulch and bluff,
  And her hair blows wild and wide.

" Sit fast, sit fast by me, sweetheart !
   The bank is steep to ride ! "—
The bank is steep for a strong man's leap,
   And her eyes are staring wide.

" Sit fast, sit fast by me, sweetheart !
   The Run is swift to ride ! "
The Run is swift with mountain drift,
   And she sways from side to side.

Is it a wash of the yellow moss,
   Or a drift of the autumn's gold,
The mountain torrent foams across
   For the dead pine's roots to hold?

Is it the bark of the sycamore,
   Or bark of the white birch-tree,
The mountaineer on the other shore
   Hath followed and still can see ?

No mountain moss or leaves, my heart !
   No bark of birchen gray !—
Young hair of gold and a face death-cold
   The wild stream sweeps away.

THE MOONSHINER.

HOW long we had lain and had listened !
  Where the trees let in winks of the sun,
Ere their gun-barrels glittered and glistened
  In the gully below by the run !
We had watched all the night and the morning—
  And our limbs stoven stiff with the chill
Of the dew ; but my Lise had the warning,
  And we knew all was up with the still
If we ever gave over our waiting,
  The four of us :   I and Bud Roe,
Two Tollivers—hated and hating—
  And the posse nigh twenty or so.

The evening before we had reckoned
  Their men would ride up through the glen ;
And it took little more than a second
  To say how we 'd manage it then :

For the valley wound up like an alley,
   Built blind with steep bluffs, and no trees
At the bottom ; the rest of the valley
   Scrub bush that just reached to the knees.
With me and one Tolliver watching
   In front, and Bud Roe in the gap
With a Tolliver—danger of botching ?—
   Them jumbled like rats in a trap !

So we all took a pull at the bottle
   Lise brought me that morning ; and though
We had eaten, nor left what would throttle
   An ant, we were hungry, I know,—
For the other, as hungry as quiet !
   For the first of the gang had n't reached
The gully, or hardly passed by it,
   When a wild-hawk — *they* thought it — had
      screeched.
When a pewee had whistled, we knew it
   The signal the posse were in,
Every man of them. Well, *they* would do it !
   And *we*—well, *we* had to begin !

A pistol each side and a rifle
  Or two ready loaded.   Our height
Would leave me to aim just a trifle
  To left and my pard to the right.
And we lay in the rocks, never winking,
  Just ready.—I heard the dry buzz
Of the grasshoppers ; thinking and thinking
  How solemn and silent it was :
When sudden,—I raised in a hurry,—
  The laurel whipped back—I could curse !—
Lise could n't get rid of her worry,
  And had to come there—for the worse !

Just then through the gully and thicket
  The heads of their horses and stocks
O' the Winchesters.—Click of the cricket?
  Or cocking of guns in the rocks?—
We waited until the last came in.
  I lined on the sheriff and said
"Shoot !" hoarsely ; and ushered the game in
  With the sheriff and deputy dead.
Some down ; and the other ones—very

Much taken with terror—rode back ;
Then the two in the gap made it merry
    With death-dealing crack upon crack.

And back to the open with frightened
    Wild faces the rest : and again
The guns at our shoulders were tightened :
    They spurred on us loosening the rein.
They were cornered : they saw it : and grimly
    They turned on their death ; and I leant
With my gun on the rocks, and saw dimly
    They rode at us shooting, and went
Through the smoke for the thick of our fire :
    Then Lise, who was loading my gun,
Screamed something and jumped—and a wire
    Of blood down her face : she was done.

There were six of them left, but a baby
    Could have done for me then, with *her* dead
In the stead of myself !   And it may be
    The two of us there had eat lead,
If Bud had n't come with the other—

The three were enough for the rest,
Dying hard as they did !—I would bother
With nothing, my hand on her breast,
Till they led me away, and together
Brought her to the still with the shot
In her brow.—But the buzzards will feather
And roost on the rest where they rot !

www.ingramcontent.com/pod-product-compliance
Lightning Source LLC
Chambersburg PA
CBHW021227020726
47498CB00008B/2725